Murder Under A Bridal Moon

A Mona Moon Mystery
Book Ten

Abigail Keam

Worker Bee Press

ISBN 979 8 357338 58 7
101122

Published in the USA by

Worker Bee Press
P.O. Box 485
Nicholasville, KY 40340

Books By Abigail Keam

Josiah Reynolds Mysteries
Death By A HoneyBee I
Death By Drowning II
Death By Bridle III
Death By Bourbon IV
Death By Lotto V
Death By Chocolate VI
Death By Haunting VII
Death By Derby VIII
Death By Design IX
Death By Malice X
Death By Drama XI
Death By Stalking XII
Death By Deceit XIII
Death By Magic XIV
Death By Shock XV
Death By Chance XVI
Death By Poison XVII
Death By Greed XVIII

1

"Ouch! You just stuck me with a pin, Violet," Mona complained, standing in front of a mirror.

"Then hold still. I can't do the alterations with you hopping about if you want this dress finished by your wedding date."

"Can't this wait until after breakfast?"

"NO! As soon as you finish breakfast, Dotty will sweep you away to your office, and I won't see you again until tea time. I want to get this done."

Mona sighed. "I wish Robert and I could just elope. This wedding nonsense is making me jumpy."

"Mr. Deatherage explained why. It would be unseemly for a duke to rush off and get married by a justice of the peace causing rumors as to why the sudden elopement." Blushing, Violet busied herself with pinning the hem of the white satin wedding dress.

Mona took in Violet's meaning. "Well, what if I was in the family way? It would be nobody's business but Robert's and mine," Mona huffed.

"Oh, Miss Mona, please don't say such things. Your reputation must be protected if you are to succeed in His Grace's world and be welcomed in society."

"It's a bunch of twaddle, if you ask me. Half the men I deal with have mistresses on the side, and everyone knows it including the wives. Nothing happens to the men, but let an adult woman express a healthy interest in sex, then everyone is shocked. Ridiculous."

"I see. Then it is all right for me to . . ."

Mona swiftly twirled around. "Don't you dare."

Laughing, Violet said, "So, it's do as I say and not as I do?"

Mona grinned. "Precisely. I'm beginning to agree with your mother that you should be accompanied by a chaperone on your dates."

"You're a hypocrite, Miss Mona."

"Yes, I am."

Violet put in the last pin. "There." She stood back and studied her creation.

Mona looked in the mirror pleased that the gown accented her platinum hair, pale skin, and amber eyes. "It's a beautiful dress, Violet. Simple and elegant." She studied the white, satin gown with long sleeves and a V-shaped neckline, form fitting to the waist and then flared out from the hips.

Violet commented, "I'm happy with it. Glad that you are, too. I think it shows off your figure."

Mona turned to and fro in front of the floor-length mirror to admire the dress. "What type of veil have you picked out for me?"

"I'll bring several and let you choose. I think it should be one that can be attached to your tiara and trails to the floor." Violet began unfastening the pearl buttons.

"Sounds a little heavy to me."

"Since the tiara belonged to His Grace's mother, it would honor her and could be the *something borrowed*. Officially, it won't belong to

3

ABIGAIL KEAM

you until the minister pronounces you husband and wife."

"Even then the family jewels won't belong to me as they are owned by the Brynelleth estate."

"Still, I think His Grace would be pleased that you wear something of his mother's."

Mona nodded. "I think you are right, missy. When did you get so smart?"

Violet blushed again before unlocking the bedroom door and calling for Mabelle, the upstairs maid.

"Yes, Violet?"

"Help me take this dress off, will you, Mabelle."

Mabelle's eyes lit up. "It's such a beautiful wedding gown. You happy with it, Miss Mona?"

"Indeed, I am," Mona said, putting a manicured hand on Mabelle's shoulder as she stepped out of the dress. She stood in her slip in front of the mirror studying her figure. Mona was still slender like a maiden which pleased her to no end. She had worried about consuming too many of Monsieur Bisaillon's pastries. "Hand me my frock, please."

"I can't wait for the wedding day," Mabelle

said, helping Mona get into her navy and white day outfit.

"You are coming to the reception?" Mona asked.

Mabelle looked as though she was going to swoon. "Wouldn't miss it for the world. Just think I am invited to the biggest social event of the decade. Me, a little nobody from Monkey's Eyebrow, Kentucky going to hobnob with the swells."

"You're someone to us, Mabelle. The upstairs couldn't function without you," Mona said.

"Thank you, Miss Mona. I take that to heart."

"Mabelle, pick up the hem, will ya and help me."

"Yes, Violet."

They picked up the dress and took it to a bedroom where Violet stored her sewing machine. Together they placed the dress on a mannequin, spreading the dress hem on clean sheets placed on the floor. Then they covered the dress with another clean sheet.

"Thank you, Mabelle."

"Anytime, Violet."

"Now, not a word to anyone about the design

of the dress. Outside of Miss Mona, only you have seen it."

Mabelle pantomimed locking her lips and throwing away the key over her shoulder.

Violet patted her on the back, saying, "I'm starving. Let's have breakfast. I understand Monsieur Bisaillon is making French toast this morning."

"I can't, Violet. I'm helping Dora wash windows this morning. Gotta run."

Violet protested, "You need to eat, Mabelle."

"I did earlier, but you enjoy your breakfast. I'll see you later."

"Okay, if you say so." Violet headed downstairs having no idea she would find out later something dreadful.

2

Mona was spreading jam on her toast when Dotty strode into the breakfast nook and poured herself a cup of coffee. She was followed by Chloe, Mona's white Standard Poodle.

"Good morning."

Since Mona had a mouthful of food, she responded by giving a small wave. After taking a sip of orange juice, she said, "Good morning. You look mighty chipper, Dotty."

"Most everyone has replied to your wedding invitations." She placed a stack of telegrams and letters in front of Mona.

Chloe put her head in Mona's lap, whining for a treat. She was rewarded with a piece of bacon smuggled under the table, as Mona pushed the telegrams and letters to one side so she could continue eating breakfast. "Who is coming?"

"Lady Alice and her husband will be here a week before the wedding."

Mona gleefully clapped her hands. "Oh, good. I was hoping they would come early."

"The President and Mrs. Roosevelt send their regrets, but Mrs. Roosevelt's cousin, Mrs. Longworth, is coming."

Mona nodded. "I never expected the President and the First Lady to attend. The invitation was sent out of politeness."

"The Prince of Wales declines as well, but has sent a wedding gift."

"What is it?"

"A silver framed picture of himself in his royal regalia with the inscription: 'Best wishes to Robert and Mona.'"

Mona rolled her eyes. "Thank goodness he is not coming. Robert will be relieved. There is too much drama with the Prince around."

"Viscountess Furness accepts. She hopes you will put her up during her stay."

Making a face, Mona said, "Don't these people ever spring for their own accommodations? She is Robert's friend. She can stay at his home."

"Mabel Dodge Luhan is coming with Aloha Wanderwell."

"I didn't know they were acquainted, but then Mabel knows everyone. I should have realized. Did you know that Aloha Wanderwell is the first woman to drive around the world?"

Dotty bit her lower lip before speaking. "Was it wise to invite Mrs. Wanderwell?"

Mona looked surprised. "What do you mean?"

"Well, there is a lot of scandal connected with her. Her husband was accused of being a German spy and arrested in the United States during the Great War. He started an affair with Aloha while he was still married and she was only seventeen. Then he was shot to death on his own yacht."

"I realize her life story raises some eyebrows, but so does mine. Remember, I have been accused of everything from being a Bolshevik to an atheist and then some other words one does not repeat in polite society."

"It doesn't help to associate with those who have a dark past. Birds of a feather—that kind of thing."

"Are you saying that your reputation is put at risk by me?"

"I'm saying that you should be careful."

"Dotty, that ship sailed a long time ago. I choose my friends based on their merit. Aloha is my good friend. I don't care what others think."

Looking contrite, Dotty asked, "How did you meet her?"

Petting Chloe's head, Mona said, "I encountered Aloha when she lectured in New York. It was right before I went to Mesopotamia. I was introduced by a mutual friend since we have the same interests, and we've corresponded ever since. She is a fascinating woman. You know she went to the Amazon looking for Percy Fawcett."

"Yeah, but she didn't find him, did she?"

"Gee, Dotty, when did you last go looking for a lost explorer in the uncharted jungle?"

Dotty held up her hand. "I get it. You admire this woman, but tell me—is her real name Aloha?"

"No, it's Idris Welsh." Mona pondered for a moment. "I haven't spoken to her in some time. Not since the trial for her husband's murderer. We have a lot to catch up on."

"Well, they are both coming." Dotty took a sip of coffee and put the cup down. "One more question."

"Shoot, no pun intended."

Dotty made a quick face. "I thought Harriet Fisher was the first woman to drive around the world."

Mona laughed. "It was discovered that Fisher had someone else drive, so the luster dulled a bit, but she's considered the first woman to circumnavigate the world in a car. Aloha gets the credit of being the first woman to *drive* around the world." Mona wiped her mouth and folded her napkin. "Anyone else?"

"Belle Brezing sends her regrets."

"I knew she wouldn't come, but I wanted to invite her anyway."

"This is what I'm talking about—inviting one of the nation's most notorious whores to your wedding. Thank goodness, she declined. The papers would have had a field day with that one."

"You should meet her, Dotty. She's a fascinating woman. Very well read and knows everyone and everything going on in town. She's a fountain of information—past and present."

"Thank you, but I'll pass. Miss Belle wants you to come see her soon. She wishes to give your wedding gift in person."

"How do you know?"

"She sent a telegram," Dotty replied, showing it to Mona.

Mona made a mental note. "Okay. I will visit her. Can you phone and see if I can visit soon?"

"Sure." Dotty made a note of the call and thumbed through her acceptance list. "A Mr. Zhang is coming. Who is he?"

"He was my landlord when I lived in the Chinatown section of New York City."

"He's Chinese?"

"Yes."

"I'll see if there is a hotel that will house Mr. Zhang during his stay."

Mona looked at Dotty in surprise. "Make a reservation for him at the Phoenix Hotel like everyone else. How many rooms have we booked?"

"Seven suites and thirty single rooms that can sleep two. You know they have a policy concerning non-white patrons."

"If the management gives you any guff, tell them that if they don't give my friend a nice room and treat him with the utmost courtesy, I will pull my business from them forever and give it to the Lafayette Hotel. Also, send Mr. Zhang a train ticket. I will pay for his trip and hotel. It's the least I can do, considering I used to borrow money from Mr. Zhang when I was broke. He was a good friend to me alone in the big city after my mother died. He rented me an awful apartment—more of a room with a kitchenette, but it was clean and the man looked out for me. I never had to worry about my things being stolen—not that I had much."

"Okay, but if the Phoenix protests, I'll tell them to expect a nasty phone call from you or His Grace."

"Noted. Let's move on."

"That's it for the morning post. We should get the bulk of responses in the next several days."

"Anything else?"

"Mr. Deatherage wants to see you."

"I can meet Dexter at his office later today. Find out when Belle can see me please."

"Will do, boss." Dotty stuck a pencil behind her ear. "Oh, one more thing. Your Aunt Melanie and her new beau are here."

"What!" Mona looked at her wristwatch. "It's early, even for her. What does Melanie want?"

"Something about your wedding date. I've put them in the parlor."

"Why couldn't you tell them I wasn't here?"

Dotty smirked. "You might as well get this over with. Just rip the bandage off."

Mona folded her napkin and sat it on the table. "No matter how much it hurts?"

"They're waiting. I'll have tea sent in."

"No, don't. I just want to hear what Melanie wants and have them leave." Reluctantly, Mona rose and went to the parlor at the front of Moon Manor. Opening the double doors and with Chloe trotting close behind, Mona strode in. "Good morning, Melanie. Enzo. Trust you both are feeling well."

A tall, well-built man with a pencil-thin mustache rose to his feet and kissed Mona's hand. He was immaculately dressed in a pin-striped, double-breasted navy suit with a white linen handkerchief peeking from his left chest pocket. He smelled of expensive cologne and drugstore pomade. "Good morning, Senorita. I am very well, thank you." He glanced at Chloe, who had planted herself by his legs and looked up at him expectantly.

14

"Please sit down, Enzo." Noticing the dog bothered him, Mona ordered, "Come here, Chloe. So sorry. She doesn't bite. Chloe just wanted a pet."

"Does she have to pant so loud?" Melanie complained. "She's drooling."

Irritated with her visitors, Mona rang a bell and when Samuel, the butler-in-training under Mr. Thomas, appeared, she said, "Please take Chloe to the kitchen and give her a treat."

Watching the dog leave with Samuel, Enzo took his seat next to Melanie, Mona's aunt, although they were only a few years apart in age. They had the same hair coloring with Melanie's being just a shade darker and the same pale skin, but that's where the similarities ended. Mona cared about her fellow man while Melanie cared about . . . well, Melanie.

Mona took a seat across from them. "You wanted to see me?"

Melanie pouted. "I've only had a few moments with you since your return from Brynelleth. Hardly a chance to talk."

"I've been busy."

"No doubt with your wedding plans, but

you've butted into my life."

"Oh? How so?"

Melanie reached for Enzo's hand and clasped it. "I hated you for forcing me on that South American cruise, but then I met Enzo and everything changed. I'm so glad I went now."

"You didn't have a choice," Mona said dryly.

"Must you be so blunt? It's crude," Melanie sniffed, making a clicking sound with her teeth. "Anyway, Enzo and I have decided to get married."

"Congratulations," Mona said, not surprised that Melanie wanted to marry a gigolo she had dragged from Brazil.

"We thought it a good idea if we piggybacked onto your wedding and got married at the same time—a double wedding. It would save a lot of fuss and bother."

"Not to mention money," Mona quipped.

"Well, I'm sure money is not a concern for you."

Mona rose. Unfortunately, she saw this coming. It was either work with Melanie or have her aunt start a shadow whispering campaign behind her back. The only way to deal with Melanie was to dangle money in front of her. "I'm sorry, Melanie, but my wedding day is reserved for Robert and me alone. However, if you two wish to be married next June, I'll pay for the wedding—with a cap, of course."

Melanie blinked. "June is so far away. I want to be married soon."

"Go right ahead, but you may not share my wedding day with Robert."

"I don't see why not. Everyone will be here already—all my friends."

"All the newspaper coverage. All the folderol. All the attention. The answer is no."

"I think you're horrid, Mona," Melanie spat out.

"Very possibly I am, but Robert is a duke and you are . . . just you."

"You wouldn't dare treat me this way if your Uncle Manfred was still alive. My brother wouldn't stand for it."

Enzo turned to Melanie. "Dearest, did you not hear your niece say she'd pay for our wedding? We must rejoice. Don't pooh-pooh such a gift." He looked at Mona. "May we inquire as to the amount we may spend for our blessed day?"

"Two thousand."

Melanie huffed, "You can't put on a decent wedding for two thousand. What would our friends think?"

"Two thousand is a lot of money, Melanie," Mona said. "More than many people make in a year. These days people have a quiet church wedding with a cake and punch for the reception. You do remember there is a Depression in the country, and men have been thrown out of work?"

"I don't see you having a small wedding like the common man."

"We are hosting Bluegrass charities on our wedding day and asking invitees to bring canned food to the reception, which will be distributed by various churches. Guests have been asked to give to their favorite charities and not purchase a wedding gift."

"Not from what I've seen as wedding gifts stacked in the ballroom."

"I have to agree that guests went a little over-board on the wedding gifts. Believe me, if Robert and I could elope, we would."

"Yeah, right." Melanie narrowed her eyes,

"How about five thousand?"

Annoyed, Mona spat out, "How about you pay for your own wedding? You were given a huge stipend last year. Use that money."

"It's mostly gone."

"That's your problem then, Melanie. I told you the money would have to last a long while." Mona rubbed her temple as she was getting a headache. "What am I gonna do with you?"

"Ladies. Ladies. Let's compromise," Enzo said. "How about three thousand and we have the reception at Moon Manor with Miss Mona hosting?" He raised Melanie's clasped hand and kissed it. "What do you say, dearest?"

Melanie pressed her lips in disdain and whined, "If that's all my niece is willing to help us, I guess it is okay."

Mona stopped short of calling Melanie something rude and said instead, "I'll have Dexter Deatherage send over a contract, but you better read it carefully. I'm going to put stipulations in it."

"Can't we have the money now?" Melanie asked.

"Oh, for goodness' sake, I'm busy. See yourselves out," Mona said, walking out of the room. She ran into Samuel coming down the hallway. Pulling him aside, she said, "Samuel, make sure my guests leave the property before they steal the silver. Make sure your shirt is still on your back when they leave."

"Your aunt here?"

Mona nodded. "With her awful beau. Get rid of them."

"Leave it to me, Miss Mona. I'll make sure they depart with smiles on their faces."

"You are so good at telling people to go to hell without them realizing it. I'll leave my aunt in your capable hands."

"Yes, Miss Mona. I'll take care of those two," Samuel said, before going into the parlor.

As Mona headed for her office, she heard Samuel cry in a booming voice, "Put that silver candy dish down, please!"

Realizing that Samuel must have caught the two pilfering the silver, Mona gave a short laugh. She knew he would put those two grifters out on their ears soon enough, and she would be able to start her day.

That's what she thought, but it turned out differently.

3

Mona and Dotty worked all morning until all needed correspondence was completed. Dotty had signed contracts to return to Dexter Deatherage and several telegrams to send off after lunch. She didn't mind going into town. It was a welcomed break from the drudgery of office toil.

Mona cleaned her desk, putting copies of the letters in the safe while Dotty burned discarded notes in the fireplace. This was common practice for Mona, who feared employees learning corporate secrets. Looking at her wristwatch, Mona said, "A half-hour till lunch. I think I'll take a walk. Stretch my legs a bit."

"Better check the weather. It was threatening to rain when I walked over." Dotty lived in a four-room cottage on the Moon estate.

Mona went to a window and opened it, poking her head outside. It smelled like rain and the leaves on the trees reached upward to the darkening sky. She could hear a tractor in the distance, the kitchen screen door slamming shut, crows cawing as they flew by overhead, and the clippety-clop of horses' hooves on concrete as two pregnant mares were being moved to another pasture taking the short cut across Moon Manor's driveway. Mona waved to the grooms escorting the horses. The men cheerfully waved back. It was a normal fall day comprised of normal sounds, normal smells, and normal human interactions.

"The trees are turning. Those water maples are going to be bright red this year," Mona mentioned, "and a storm does look like it's heading our way."

"Told you so."

"Are you staying for lunch?"

"I'm going to pass today. I want to get these telegrams off. I can get a sandwich at the drugstore."

"Take a Pinkerton with you."

"Don't I always. I know the protocol."

"Will you be taking that handsome Pinkerton with the ginger hair?"

Dotty blushed. "Noticed, have you?"

"How can one not? That red head of his is so bright, it looks like his head is on fire from a distance."

"He's from Viking stock, you know."

Mona said, "I would say so, especially with a name like Gunderson. Yes, he is easy on the eyes—square jaw, broad shoulders, narrow waist. Good luck with him."

A knock sounded on the door.

"Come in," Mona said.

Mr. Thomas, the head butler, and Dora, the downstairs maid, entered the room.

Mona could tell from their sober expressions that something was wrong.

Mr. Thomas, an elderly black man with a dignified bearing and graying hair, announced, "I'm sorry to bother you, Miss Mona, but we seem to have misplaced one of our employees."

Mystified, Mona encouraged Mr. Thomas, "Go on."

"We can't find Mabelle," Mr. Thomas said.

"She has disappeared."

"That's not good," Mona replied. "What were her duties this morning?"

Dora spoke up. "She was to help me wash the downstairs windows. We were to do the insides and then all the mirrors. Mabelle never showed up to help."

"Maybe she took sick and went home," Dotty offered.

"No, Miss," Mr. Thomas said. "She would never leave Moon Manor without informing me."

"Has the house been searched?" Mona asked. "Maybe she fell and is injured."

Mr. Thomas said, "We've searched and she is not in the house."

"I just heard the kitchen screen door slam shut," Mona offered.

"That was Obadiah heading to the chicken coop to look for Mabelle," Mr. Thomas replied.

"She wouldn't be there. The upstairs maid has no reason to mess with the chickens." Mona was concerned. She agreed with Mr. Thomas that Mabelle would never leave without telling someone. "Let's not panic. I'm sure there is a simple explanation."

Mr. Thomas said, "Let's hope so."

"Let's track the last person to see Mabelle. I spoke with her this morning myself. Check with Violet. I know Mabelle was helping her this morning."

"I have spoken with Miss Violet and she said Mabelle left her in the sewing room around eight-thirty. Said she was going downstairs to help Dora."

Baffled, Mona asked, "Is there any reason she might have gone to His Grace's home? Maybe Monsieur Bisaillon wanted her to borrow something."

Mr. Thomas said, "I'll ask."

"Have you checked the swimming pool?" Dotty asked.

Mona felt her heart clutch tightly.

"What's going on?" Robert Farley, Duke of Brynelleth, walked through the door and passed Mr. Thomas and Dora. While noting the concern on Mona's face, he gave her a quick peck on the cheek. "Is something wrong? May I help? You all have the most serious expressions on your faces."

"We are missing Mabelle," Mona replied. She felt relieved that Robert was with her. "Have you seen her?"

"She's the upstairs maid? Late thirties, dark hair, dark eyes, wears her hair in a bun?" Robert asked.

"Yes," Mr. Thomas answered.

Robert shook his head. "I saw her talking to a man in the garden this morning, but not since then."

Mr. Thomas asked, "What man, Your Grace?"

Robert said, "I'm sorry, Thomas. I couldn't see his face."

"Was he an employee?" Mona asked.

"I don't think so. He was wearing a dark suit, polished shoes, and had brownish hair, but his back was turned to me."

Mona said, "The outfit narrows it down from those who wear bib overalls, uniforms, and working pants. That cuts out local farmers, law enforcement, milkmen, mailmen, and horse farm employees. Sounds like a professional person from Lexington."

"Or a horse farm owner or even a Pinkerton, darling."

Mona huffed. "I hardly think so."

Robert raised an eyebrow. "You might want to reconsider after what we've been through.

Let's not forget what happened at Brynelleth."

Pausing for a moment, Mona re-evaluated. Maybe Robert was right. Even though she and Robert had the help of Great Britain's MI5, MI6, and William Donovan, Roosevelt's secret spy, they had a tough time of it at Brynelleth. The thought was ridiculous though. They didn't even know if Mabelle was really missing. She could be at her home with a bad toothache. Still–with all the trouble she and Robert had at his ancestral home with a Pinkerton and a German assassin several months ago put a bad taste in Mona's mouth. "Were they arguing?"

"Mabelle seemed excited, but they weren't arguing that I could tell. I'm sorry, Mona. I didn't pay more attention as I don't eavesdrop on servants' tittle-tattle."

Mona hid her disappointment. Robert had the typical English attitude of reserved apathy toward servants while she considered many employees as part of her family. Violet, Mr. Thomas, Samuel, and Jamison were very dear to her, and she would go to any length to protect them. While she was not very close to Mabelle, the woman was her employee and Mona felt responsible for her. She directed her instructions to Mr. Thomas. "Have Mr. Mott search the grounds and question all employees if they have seen Mabelle today. Tell Samuel to search Moon Manor and Mabelle's cottage again. If we can't find her within the hour, reach out to her family. Maybe they've heard something, but I don't want to alarm them until we're sure Mabelle is actually missing."

Mr. Thomas answered, "I understand, but Mabelle doesn't have any family. She's alone in the world, but don't worry, Miss Mona. We'll find her."

Mona sighed with relief. She knew Mr. Thomas and Mr. Mott would scour Mooncrest Farm searching for Mabelle, leaving no stone unturned until they found her.

And find her, they did, two hours later. Behind the mare barn.

4

Five days later, Mona was met at the front door of Moon Manor by Samuel, who took her hat and coat. Behind Mona trudged Violet and Willie Deatherage, dressed in black and wearing black armbands with the Mooncrest Farm emblem.

He looked sympathetically at the three gloomy women.

"I'll keep my purse. Thank you, Samuel," Willie said. She peeked outside to see what was keeping her husband, Dexter Deatherage. He was Mona's attorney and right-hand man when it came to Moon Enterprises, which was a conglomerate of many businesses including copper mines. She spied Dexter huddled in the driveway with Robert Farley and Mr. Mott, the head of Mona's Pinkerton security.

Samuel closed the front door shutting off Willie's view. "I'll bring some refreshments."

Mona replied, "That would be nice, Samuel." She drifted into the parlor where a small fire was lit. Standing by the fireplace, she warmed her hands, murmuring, "Got a bit chilly. I think fall weather is finally here."

Violet and Willie took seats in chairs facing the fire.

"The days are still very temperate," Willie said, "but I did think it was cooler this morning. Will have to get out my sweaters soon."

Violet moved away from the fire, thinking it was too warm for one. She was not convinced that fall had arrived. Nevertheless, the fire was cheerful as she watched Mona restlessly pace about the room.

Mona angrily said, "I don't know why I have all this security if something like this can happen in broad daylight on Mooncrest Farm."

"It's not your fault," Willie said.

"Isn't it?" Mona snapped back. "I'm supposed to provide a safe work environment for my workers, especially the women." Mona threw herself in a chair. "This is just awful. The entire town is in an uproar."

Violet said, "That's because the local papers are sensationalizing the murder."

"Somehow a rumor of Mabelle meeting a man got out. Of course, they hint at Robert."

Willie said, "Robert's name is never mentioned in connection with Mabelle."

Mona shot back. "His name doesn't have to be mentioned. Just implied."

"I don't understand why Mabelle was outside the house and at the mares' barn of all places," Violet commented. "She said she was going to help Dora."

Willie added, "Dora swears she did not see Mabelle leave the house, and she was washing windows in the front rooms. She would have seen her if Mabelle left by the front door."

"It's a mystery, Willie, for sure," Mona said. "Someone lured poor Mabelle to the mares' barn, strangled her, and then stuffed her broken body into one of the horse trailers. Her murderer had to be a very strong man to lift Mabelle's body and carry her. She was found under a pile of feed sacks in the back of a trailer."

"Yeah, Mabelle was a big girl. Weighing about

one-fifty," Violet mused.

"Big, but not fat. Mabelle was strong, but she had no defensive wounds," Mona said. "I don't see how she was overpowered and why. Who would want to hurt Mabelle?"

Robert and Dexter strolled into the room just as Samuel came through another door, pushing a tea cart.

Dexter asked, "Any chance for some coffee, Samuel?"

Samuel pointed to a big pot. "Right here, sir. I've got tea, little cakes, and sandwiches. People need to eat after a funeral. Lifts their spirits." He placed the food on a little table set up previously.

"Thank you, Samuel. Very thoughtful. I think we can all do with a little something," Mona said, pouring coffee into porcelain cups and handing them over to Dexter and Robert. She poured tea for herself, Violet, and Willie.

"I'll take two," Willie said, referring to lumps of sugar.

After Mona finished pouring, Samuel put the coffee and tea pots on the table with the food, along with extra cups. He knew people might stop by.

Feeling a bit overwhelmed, Mona said, "Everyone—help yourselves."

"I'll get you a plate, Mona," Robert offered. "I know what you like."

"Thank you, darling," Mona said in a defeated voice.

Robert took notice of her listless tone, but didn't comment. He got her a plate of several lemon tarts, little turkey and roast beef sandwiches with the crust cut off, and a walnut brownie, which Monsieur Bisaillon made especially for Mona. He handed the plate to Mona with a napkin. "Violet, what can I get you?"

"Anything. I'm starving."

"Righto. Grub coming up," Robert replied with a grin.

Violet returned a ghost of a smile at Robert's use of an American expression, but like Mona, she looked sadly somber.

Robert was concerned about both women.

Dexter handed a plate to his wife, Willie, and sat on the couch next to her chair.

"Thank you, Dexter," she said, putting the plate on a side table. "I'll eat in a moment."

"Suit yourself," he said, laying his plate of

food on his lap. He was hungry and picked up a roast beef sandwich. What he really wanted was a steak and buttery baked potato, but this would suffice for now.

Robert pulled up a stool and sat next to Mona. "This fire feels good. There was a chill in the air this morning."

Mona asked, "Robert, did you speak with the sheriff?"

"Both Mr. Mott and I spoke with him. There are no specific suspects, but every man who was at Mooncrest Farm that morning is under suspicion."

"That's what I was afraid of. Any chance of the sheriff solving this murder soon?"

Robert said, "He and Mr. Mott are interviewing all male employees. They'll find their man."

"Are we sure it was a man who killed Mabelle?" Violet asked.

"I don't see a woman having the strength to strangle a woman as strong as Mabelle," Willie answered. "They found the bruising of handprints on her neck, so someone manually choked the life out of her. You have to have muscular hands to do that."

"Oh, Willie, do you have to be so graphic?" Mona complained.

"Sorry, Mona," Willie said. She picked up a sandwich and nibbled on it.

Mona sighed, clutching a handkerchief. "No, I'm sorry. My nerves have been raw since Mabelle was found. Perhaps if I knew how she left the house without anyone seeing would ease my mind. If someone can easily leave Moon Manor without a witness, then someone can enter as well."

"I'd say she went out the library's French doors," Robert said. "Cut through the garden over to the mares' barn."

"That's the only explanation," Mona said. "I'm going to put a bell on those doors."

"We know she didn't go through the front door, the kitchen's back door, or the servants' wing entrance door. That leaves the library's doors and the side door past the gaming room." The gaming room was where Mona allowed gentlemen to smoke, play billiards, and drink port after dinner. The room was rarely used as Robert didn't imbibe alcohol any longer as that was a condition of his marriage to Mona.

"Did Mabelle have any romantic interests?" Willie asked, now fussing with her dress hem by pulling a loose thread. "Maybe a man proposed and she turned him down. You know some men don't take rejection very well."

Violet answered, "She had a long-standing beau from town, but he has an alibi for the time of Mabelle's death. A distant cousin several times removed, I think."

"Was he at the funeral?" Willie asked.

"I didn't see him, which I thought was odd," Violet said, getting up to pour herself another cup of tea. "I understand he was torn up about her death."

Mona stood.

Everyone looked expectantly at her.

Violet held the teapot toward her. "Another cup?"

"I'm afraid I have a hellish headache. You all stay and enjoy the refreshments. The kitchen staff went out of their way to prepare this repast, but I'm going to bed."

Robert said, "I'll follow you up, Mona."

"There's no need."

"I want to. I just need to speak with Dexter

before I check in on you."

"All right. Willie, I'll call you later."

Willie stood as well. "Take an aspirin, Mona, and close the curtains in your room. The darkness will help to ease the tension in your forehead."

Mona nodded and went up the grand staircase, leaving the four behind.

As soon as Mona was out of earshot, Willie asked Robert, "What gives?"

"She's been moody ever since Mabelle was found."

Dexter said, "That's so unlike Mona. She's stumbled upon dead bodies before and never missed a beat." He stole a look at Violet. "Do you know?"

"I think everyone is a little sad about Mabelle's death. I know I'm concerned and a little frightened, too."

Robert asked, "You think Mona is frightened? I've never known that woman to be frightened of anything."

Violet added, "I think Miss Mona is not only concerned about the murder, but the proximity to her wedding day. It's making her sick with worry."

"It's just a coincidence—the proximity I mean."

"Her Aunt Melanie and her beau were here that morning, making subtle threats and coercing Miss Mona out of money," Violet said. "I was upstairs working when they were here, but Miss Mona later told me about their visit."

Stunned, Robert angrily turned to Dexter. "This is the first I have heard about this. Dexter, can you enlighten me?"

Knowing that Robert's anger had a hair trigger when it came to Mona, Dexter calmly explained, "Melanie is going to marry that gold digger from South America and wants Mona to foot the bill for their wedding."

"Sounds like blackmail to me."

"It can be viewed as that, but Mona just wanted to get rid of them by dangling a carrot in front of them. Melanie fancied to get married with the two of you on your wedding day, but Mona insisted that she marry in June of next year."

Robert ran his hand through his hair. "Melanie is such a pest. She drives Mona natty always wanting this and that."

Dexter suggested, "We can put a restraining

order on Melanie not to have further contact with Mona."

"It would make the papers and cause a scandal. It would be twisted around to make Mona look stingy and cruel. Melanie is always going to be a boil on someone's backside, might as well be us," Robert replied.

Reluctantly, Willie put her cup down on the side table. She could tell Robert was anxious to be with Mona. "We should be going. The sooner we get back into our usual routines, the better so everyone can put this dreadful event behind us."

Robert said, "We can't put it behind us until we catch the murderer. If we don't, everyone will pepper us with questions and suspicions—and I can just see what the newspapers will print."

"Has anyone declined their wedding invitation?" Dexter asked.

Robert answered, "On the contrary, most everyone has accepted. People like nothing better than to experience schadenfreude."

Willie said, "Gesundheit."

Robert smiled at Willie's joke. "Very cute."

Dexter pulled Willie to her feet. "We're going. When my wife starts cracking jokes, I know it's time to leave."

"I just said we should leave. Quit making it your idea," Willie complained. She turned to Violet and Robert. "Dexter makes it sound like everything is his idea."

Dexter said to Robert, "Get ready, old chap. Marriage is less about love and more about who is right."

Willie pooh-poohed her husband. "Quit filling Robert's head with your nonsense."

"See what I mean." He prodded Willie toward the foyer. "Let's get your coat and hat, girlie."

Robert and Violet grinned at each other. Everyone knew Dexter worshipped Willie, and they were very happy with each other.

Robert saw them to the door and watched them leave, waving goodbye from the portico. Then he bounded up the stairs to Mona.

5

Robert knocked on Mona's bedroom door.

"Come in."

He entered the suite and went over to Mona lying on the bed with Chloe snuggling beside her. "May I get you anything?"

"I'm fine"

"You don't seem fine. You left your bedroom door unlocked. Don't you think that unwise with a killer on the loose?" He took off his jacket and tossed it on a chair.

"Oh, Robert, please don't scold me. I don't want to be lectured."

"You've lectured me often enough."

Mona turned toward him and smiled. "I have, haven't I? Is that what I've become—a scold?"

Robert returned to the door and locked it.

"There. Now we can fight in private."

"You didn't answer my question. Have I turned into a scold?"

"You are a magnificent goddess whom I'm going to marry in a few weeks. Nothing is going to stop that, so tell me what the matter is." He put Chloe on the floor and jumped on the bed next to Mona, gathering her in his powerful arms. "Talk, Mona. You can trust me, darling."

Mona laid her head on his shoulder and thrust her hand inside his shirt next to his skin. The feel of his warm flesh comforted her as she inhaled his smell. "I feel guilty."

"About what?"

"I think I brought this trouble back from Brynelleth."

"You think Sicherheitsdienst agents are sneaking about the Bluegrass and killing upstairs maids?"

"Yes, I do." Mona pulled away from Robert, leaning on her elbows. "Robert, I want to sell the copper mines. It's the copper that is causing all this trouble. Let's get rid of the mines."

"I'm surprised. You told me that it was your patriotic duty to keep those mines. Now you want to chuck them?"

"I'm tired of all the drama and the innocent getting killed. We were followed the entire trip to Brynelleth by German agents trying to get me to sell the copper and then when I wouldn't, they tried to kill me and you. It's just not worth it to keep those mines. I'm having to look over my shoulder all the time."

"Mona, I hate to tell you, but all great men and women of any industry—the thinkers of our time face the same problems. There are always nefarious persons who will steal, coerce, black-mail, or murder to get what they want."

"The cost to our friends and family is too high. I wonder if I am up to it."

Tongue-in-cheek, Robert said, "You have several options—you can turn Moon Enterprises over to Melanie and walk away. We'd be paupers, but I'll take your hand in marriage even if you are poor."

"You said there were several options."

"You can sell the mines alone, but they make up the bulk of the Moon Enterprises' fortune and again, we'd live like paupers. I'll still marry you."

"And?"

"We fight back. Keep what is good in Moon Enterprises and throw out the bad when we can and if we can. Darling, take a hard gaze about you. We are not the only ones faced with such difficulties during this very desperate time, but can't you see all the good you have done?"

"Have I?"

"Ah, now, you are fishing for compliments."

Mona chuckled.

"I'm serious, my American cow. You pay good wages to your employees. Look at the families you have helped rise from destitution. Your employees are well-fed, enjoy free medical care, and their kids go to school wearing shoes. Look at Violet. She never would have finished school if you hadn't influenced her, and she's talking about going to some fashion academy now. You support a woman's right to control her finances without a male overseer. Your bank catering to women is the number one bank in the Bluegrass. You have given out the most loans at lower interest rates and still the bank is making money. Mona, really—you have helped so many people."

"Then why am I hated so? People call me

horrible names—say my policies are un-Christian."

"I don't think Jesus would agree with these naysayers."

"Then why do they curse me?"

"Because that's how the game is played. Come on. You're a big girl now. There are men in this world, who can't stand the regular Joe having a good life. These men have always gotta be stepping on someone. Makes them feel important, and they are usually standing behind a flag or a Bible to knock the other guy down. Don't let these people take your dreams away. You said you knew what it was to be down on your luck."

"Yes, I know what it is to be broke and not knowing when I was going to eat my next meal. If people hadn't come to my aid, I never would have made it. I feel a need to help others like I was supported."

"See. I told you so. Now move over. You're hogging the bed."

"You're not even supposed to be here. What if the newspapers find out and print that you were in my bedroom?"

"Most men in this town would salute me and buy me a drink. Now, shut up and move over. We both need some rest. It's been taxing the last five days."

"But . . .?"

"Quit whining, Mona. Let's take a lie down. We'll deal with this nonsense later."

For once Mona acquiesced. Robert was right. Realizing that she was being a silly willy, Mona was thankful for Robert. He always set her straight as she did him.

They made a good pair. Mona snuggled closer to Robert dreaming of their life together. She loved him. She needed him. She desired him. She ached for him. No man had ever lit the fire in her like Robert did. Mona felt it was important she marry him. It was a gut feeling she couldn't explain except that it felt right—like thread going through a needle.

Mona looked forward to the life they would share.

She was sure it wouldn't be dull.

6

Mona woke up mid-day to a sunny afternoon. She looked about the room, but Robert had left, leaving a note on her dresser. It stated he would join her for dinner. Mona had no appointments that day, so she decided to visit Belle Brezing. She rang the staff dining room where she knew Jamison, her chauffeur, would be sitting reading the paper. Would he be at the front door in fifteen?

Yes, he would be right there with the car.

Mona washed her face, combed her hair, and put on fresh lipstick. Her dress was rumpled after her nap, so she changed into another black dress with red piping, red collar, and red cloth buttons sewn down the front. After putting on her black arm band, she picked up fresh black gloves and

ABIGAIL KEAM

her purse. Mona then bounded down the stairs
and went in search of Mr. Thomas. Finding him
in the butler pantry, she told him that she was
visiting Miss Belle and would be home by early
evening.

"Make sure you make it home for dinner.
Fried chicken, mashed potatoes, the last of the
fresh peas, corn pudding, and peach ice cream for
dessert. If you eat the chicken with your hands,
I'll never tell." It always entertained Mr. Thomas
when Mona's European friends ate fried chicken
with a knife and fork.

"Please don't let His Grace talk Monsieur
Bisaillon into making mushy peas."

Mr. Thomas made a face. Mona could tell he
found mushy peas not worthy of gracing Moon
Manor's table. "I'll have the cook make mushy
peas from canned peas for His Grace and you
can have the fresh peas. Marriage is all about
compromise, Miss Mona. Might as well start
now."

"Thank you, Mr. Thomas. A perfect solu-
tion." She put on her gloves. "Like I said, I'll be
home in a couple of hours. You will give Robert
the message?"

"Yes, Miss. Remember to go in the back way. You don't want people seeing you go in the front door of Belle's place."

Mona affectionately patted Mr. Thomas on the shoulder. "I'll do my best not to embarrass my folks."

Mr. Thomas didn't reply, but knew Mona included the house staff and farm employees in her definition of *folks*. That's why he loved her so. She wasn't a rich white employer to him. She was the daughter he never had. There was a quiet understanding between the two of them that nothing could rend asunder. "Best be going if you want to be back before the gong rings."

Mona hurried to the car where Jamison waited patiently for her. He opened the car door for her, and they scurried quickly out the front gate before the Pinkertons knew they were gone. The last thing she needed was lonely, aggressive men with guns following her to a whorehouse.

7

Mona waited in Belle's sitting room. The room hadn't been dusted for a long time and books lay helter-skelter on bookshelves and the floor. Photographs of Belle in her heyday with prominent men of Lexington hung crooked on the walls. She wondered if Belle was still letting long-time customers patronize the house. Surely not if the rest of the house was in this same state, but this room was Belle's private sitting room. The other rooms might not have been in such poor shape.

The door opened and Belle walked in using a cane. "So nice to see you, my dear."

Mona rose from her chair and went to greet Belle, kissing her on the cheek.

"How have you been? I haven't seen you

since you returned from England."

"I've been busy as you well know." Mona put her arm around Belle. "I want to talk with you about something. Won't you please come to my wedding?"

Belle let Mona ease her into a chair. "That's very sweet of you to invite me, but you know I can't. The papers would have a field day with it—a famous madam in a church attending a duke's wedding. Goodness. Hell might freeze over."

"Your reputation isn't worse than some of the other people who have been invited."

"It's true that ugly buildings and old whores grow respectable with age, but I'm too fond of you to take the chance."

"Then you insist on being stubborn. Will you at least let me save some wedding cake and bring it to you?"

"Only if you bring the handsome Robert Farley with you."

Mona grinned. "I think I can convince Lord Bob to come along with me."

Belle leaned back in her chair. "That would be nice." She paused, closing her eyes.

Wondering if Belle was falling asleep, Mona

asked, "Would you like me to read to you, Belle?"

Belle popped open her eyes and pointed to a corner. "There are some books on the stand next to the window. I've saved them for you as a wedding gift."

Mona went over to the stand where there were three books. They were first editions— Charles Dickens' *David Copperfield* and Wilkie Collins' *The Moonstone*. Mona perused the last book. It was a signed copy of Willa Cather's *My Antonia*. "These are for me?"

"Yes, I want you to have them."

"Thank you, Belle. I will treasure them always."

"Have you read Willa Cather's work?"

"No, I haven't had the pleasure."

"Her work is rather like the Great Plains she writes about. Bleak, monotonous, and lyrical at the same time. You can hear the wind blow over the prairie grass in her work. She is an acquired taste. You need to read something besides mysteries."

Mona teased, "Hey now. Don't knock Agatha Christie and Dorothy L. Sayers."

Belle reached for a handkerchief she kept in

her cleavage and coughed. "So sorry. I can't get rid of this blasted cold."

"Shall I ring for Pearl?"

"No, just pour me some bourbon, will ya?"

Mona poured the golden liquid into a glass.

"More, honey. You trying to starve me?"

Mona poured a hefty glass of bourbon plus a small one for herself and saluted. "May we be in heaven half an hour before the devil knows we're dead."

Belle held up her glass as well. "Here's to those who wish us well. And those that don't can go to hell."

"I'll drink to that," Mona said, cheerfully. She knocked back a stiff one.

Belle studied Mona, who wiped her chin with her hand. "Life been rough for you lately?"

"You may say so."

Belle rested her glass on her knee. "I've heard some things."

"I thought you might have."

"Pearl goes to church with Mabelle's third cousin once removed. He said that a newspaper reporter from the *Wall Street Journal* had come into town early and was greasing a lot of palms to get a story on you and your future husband. Something about Robert not being solvent and marrying you for your money."

Mona didn't like the sound of a reporter snooping around. "May I speak with Pearl?"

"By all means."

Mona rang a bell. A woman with graying hair pinned up, bulging green eyes, and sharp features opened the sitting room door. "You need something?"

"I'd like to ask a few questions, Pearl. Miss Belle says you heard something at church regarding Mabelle, my maid."

Pearl glanced at Belle who gave an imperceptible nod. "She told her cousin that a reporter was hounding her for your personal letters or a copy of your bank statement."

"Did she give the man's name?"

"No."

"Did she give her cousin a description of the man?"

"No, except the cousin said that the man paid Mabelle for information."

Mona was aghast. "I don't believe it."

"Then explain why twenty crisp five-dollar

bills were found in her cottage. Her cousin says she had this money."

"No money was found in Mabelle's cottage."

Pearl sneered, "Better check with your bully boys. I say they did find money. If you don't know about it, that means they stole it. The money should go to her kinfolk. Mabelle paid a big enough price for it."

Mona was distraught. The Pinkertons searched Mabelle's cottage before the sheriff arrived. If money was missing, that meant they had taken it. "Did she tell her cousin that she took money from this reporter?"

"I'm saying all I'm gonna say."

"Can I get in touch with this cousin?"

"I'll tell him. If he wants to see you, he'll contact you."

Belle said, "Thank you, Pearl. That's all."

The woman left the room in a sulk.

"I get the very non-subtle gist that Pearl does not approve of me," Mona said.

"Envy is a horrible taskmaster. It turns the nicest people into snakes." Belle took a sip of her bourbon before saying, "If the story about the money is true, I wouldn't be angry with Mabelle.

One hundred dollars is a lot of money for a maid."

"I *paid* Mabelle a lot of money to be an upstairs maid. She lived on Mooncrest Farm rent free. I'm sorry if I feel hot about this, but I do."

"Mabelle was a spinster doing menial work while watching other people wallow in wealth. You can hardly blame her, Mona, but the money may have been saved from Mabelle's wages. Find out the truth first before you pop a cork. This distant cousin could be making stuff up."

Mona rose from her chair and gathered her books.

"Leaving so soon?"

"I'm going to the Phoenix Hotel and track this reporter down." She paused for a moment. "I shan't see you for a while. Do you mind?"

"What can I do about it?" Resigned to loneliness, Belle took another sip of her bourbon.

"Will you at least let me save you a piece of my wedding cake?"

"Bring the delicious Robert Farley when you come next. I will welcome you both and eat your stale piece of wedding cake."

"I shall." Mona kissed Belle on the cheek. "Bye, Belle."

"Take care, sweet girl."

Mona left the room cradling her books and took the hallway leading to the kitchen. There she met Jamison, who was finishing a fried baloney sandwich and a Coca-Cola. After Mona threw two dollars on the kitchen table, they left together by the back door.

Once in the car, Mona directed, "Take me to the Phoenix, Jamison."

"You gonna bust some heads, Miss Mona? You got that look. I can always tell you're peeved when your eyebrows start knitting together."

Mona had to chuckle. "Find out anything in the kitchen from the help?"

"Pearl sure don't like you. She thinks you are trying to wiggle your way into Miss Belle's will."

"I suppose Pearl will end up being a significant recipient of Miss Belle's largesse."

"She's been with Miss Belle for over thirty years. She rightfully expects something and doesn't want you upsetting the apple cart."

"Anything else? Any visitors?"

"Regular gang comes to play poker once a week. That's about all."

"Does she have any girls working?"

"Nope. It's Miss Belle, Pearl, a maid, and kitchen staff now. Pearl told me that Miss Belle feels poorly."

"I noticed the house seemed in disarray."

"Miss Belle is starting to let go of this world and preparing for the next."

Mona didn't respond and looked out the window as Jamison drove four blocks to the Phoenix Hotel. It had begun to rain and people on the sidewalk dashed for cover. "Wait for me around the block," Mona said, as she got out of the car.

Jamison tipped his hat and drove on.

Mona entered the red brick hotel, looking for Jellybean Martin. She found him working in the lobby.

8

Jellybean spotted Mona before she saw him. He flashed his dark eyes to the mezzanine. Mona passed him without betraying any recognition of the wiry little man, who worked as a house detective for the hotel, posing as a menial worker for his cover. Jellybean quickly finished his work in the lobby and took the servants' stairway to the second floor open mezzanine. The Phoenix Hotel had hired Jellybean as a domestic and then promoted him to one of their house detectives when they noticed he had a certain flair for gathering information. After all, people speak freely around servants as they consider them part of the furniture.

He found Mona sitting in one of the leather chairs perusing a magazine. He cleaned ashtrays, picked up candy wrappers, and dusted the furniture until other guests enjoying the mezzanine left. Now that Mona was alone, he wandered over straightening magazines and refolding newspapers. Out of the corner of his mouth, he whispered, "What do you want?"

Flipping the pages of the Ladies' Home Journal, Mona said very quietly, "There is a reporter from the *Wall Street Journal* in town. See if he is staying here. If not, then contact the other hotels. I want that man found and his room searched."

"Looking for what?"

"His notes on a story about me and His Grace. Anything that connects him to my maid, Mabelle."

"What's his name?"

"I don't know. Check the register for anyone from New York City."

"Gonna cost you. I need cash up front for me. Got a gambling debt to pay."

"What's new?"

"I'll need more for greasing palms. Small bills preferred."

"Do you know Pearl from Belle's?"

"I know her."

"Mabelle, my maid from Moon Manor?"

Jellybean cut Mona off before she could finish her sentence. "Read about her death in the paper."

"Pearl goes to church with Mabelle's distant cousin, and he's flapping his jaws. See what he's got to say."

"You got a name?"

"She wouldn't give me one."

Jellybean frowned. "You're making this awfully hard. No names. No descriptions."

"Jellybean, you're a wizard. You'll track these men down."

The little man puffed up his chest as he was a sucker for flattery. "I'll get back to you when I have something."

Mona closed the magazine and handed it to Jellybean with a fifty-dollar bill inside.

Jellybean said in his most ingratiating voice, "Come again, Miss. I'll let you know when I need more."

Mona rose and left the hotel looking for her car.

Spying Mona on the corner, Jamison blew his horn.

Using her purse to shield her from the rain, Mona crossed the street and entered the car. Once inside, Mona looked at her wristwatch. "Oh, golly, I'm late for dinner. Hurry, Jamison, take me home."

Jamison took the most direct route home noticing that they were being followed by a black roadster. He adjusted the rearview mirror.

"I noticed them, too," Mona said, resisting the urge to turn around and look out the rear window. She pulled out a pearl-handle, snub nose revolver from her purse. "Jamison, do you still have the shotgun under the front seat?"

"Yes, Miss. We never leave without it."

Feeling more secure, Mona said, "Let's hurry home then."

"Sounds like a plan, Miss Mona."

Mona lay down in the back seat with her revolver in hand until they entered the gates of Mooncrest Farm. Jamison slammed on the brakes and Mona hopped out and hurried into the road, hoping to glimpse a plate number but the roadster sped off. Mona ran back through the closing gates.

She spoke with Burl, the gatekeeper. "I want a

record of all cars that pass by here, which you don't recognize, Burl. I want the color, type, who's driving, and plate number if you can get."

"Does that mean trucks as well?"

"If it's a go-cart or a wandering goat, I want to know about it."

Burl nodded. Like Jamison, he loved cars. Nothing would please him more than to jot down the passing vehicles. It gave him something to do beside open and close the gate for Mooncrest traffic.

Assured of Burl's tenacity, Mona got back in the car and rode up the driveway to Moon Manor. She was late for dinner. No time to dress. She would have to make-do with the outfit she had on. It would mean a lot of questions from Robert and prying from Violet.

Mona squared her shoulders and entered the mansion. Little did she know more than questions awaited her inside.

9

Samuel met Mona at the door, taking her hat and purse.

"Sorry I'm late. Is everyone in the dining room?"

"Miss Violet and His Grace are entertaining in the parlor. Mr. Thomas is serving them."

"Entertaining?"

"Yes, Miss. They've been waiting on you."

Mona's face brightened. "Oh, has Lady Alice arrived? She's early. She and Ogden weren't due until next Saturday." Before Samuel could stop her, Mona rushed into the parlor. "Alice!"

Five faces looked up in surprise at her—Robert dressed in formal attire, Violet in a soft lavender chiffon gown, and three ladies clad in tweed traveling outfits.

It took Mona a few seconds to recognize two of the women.

One of the women jumped up to give Mona a hug. "You look startled, my dear. We've given you a fright."

"I'm so sorry, Mabel, but I wasn't expecting you until the wedding," Mona replied to Mabel Dodge Luhan. "You took me by surprise."

"We won't be a bother, I promise," said another woman.

"My goodness. Hello, Aloha." Mona grabbed Aloha Wanderwell's hand and squeezed. "It's been a long time, my friend."

Aloha grinned. "It has been too long, Mona." She looked around the luxurious room and blurted, "Holy hell, Mona, you've come into your own. I remember you living in that horrid little excuse for an apartment in New York. You were lucky to have running water. Now look at you and this room. Fancy digs with white marble on the fireplace and blue velvet-covered furniture. Very calming. Speaking of your old lodging, how is Mr. Zhang?"

"He's coming to the wedding."

"You don't say. Don't that beat all?"

"And who is this?" Mona asked, turning her attention to a middle-aged, dark-haired woman sitting next to Mabel. She looked so fragile, Mona thought the woman's bones must be hollow like a bird's and feared she might take flight at any moment.

Mabel introduced the woman. "This is Georgia O'Keeffe. After the wedding she's coming with me to my place in Taos, New Mexico. We thought we'd get an early start this year on our vacation."

O'Keeffe gave Mabel a sidelong glance. "I told you that I'm only staying a few days in Taos. There's a ranch I want to visit."

Robert asked, "Which ranch is that, Miss O'Keeffe?"

"It's called Ghost Ranch. It's twenty-one thousand acres of isolation. Taos is too noisy for me. I like solitude. Actually, I've already rented a house on the property."

"Oh, Georgia. You just don't like people." Mabel looked up at Mona still standing. "Georgia is a painter. Know her work?"

Robert interjected, "I do. I admire your paintings, ma'am."

"Of course, you do, young man."

Robert raised an eyebrow at Georgia's hubris.

Aloha announced, "I'm starving, Mona. Are you going to feed us?"

"It's fried chicken for dinner."

"Sounds good to me"

"I feel quite overdressed for fried chicken," Robert said, looking down at his tux.

"So do I," piped up Violet, who was quite star struck at the sophisticated ladies sitting to the right of her. Aloha Wanderwell was a hero of hers. When she spoke, her voice trembled a bit.

"Mr. Thomas will direct you to where you ladies can freshen up. That will give Robert and Violet time to change into something more casual. We eat fried chicken with our fingers around here." Mona turned to Mr. Thomas, who was standing in a corner observing the new guests. "If you would, please."

Mr. Thomas extended his white-gloved hand. "This way, ladies."

As soon as Aloha and Georgia vanished up the staircase, Mabel grabbed Mona. "I'm so sorry about this, but Georgia was having trouble at home and wanted me to give her a ride to Taos instead of taking the train." Mabel leaned in and whispered, "Her husband is having an affair with a much younger woman, and Georgia couldn't stand it any longer. I could hardly refuse her under the circumstances."

"We'll make do, Mabel. Don't worry about it."

"You're a doll. So understanding. I wish all my friends were nice like you."

"You better freshen up, Mabel. My cook stays dinner for no one."

"Of course. See you in a jiffy." Mr. Thomas escorted Mabel up the staircase.

Looking to see that Mabel was out of earshot, Robert asked, "Did you know they were coming?"

"This early? No. But both Aloha and Mabel were coming to the wedding. I didn't think so soon. I think Mabel is telling the truth about Miss O'Keeffe. She is notoriously loyal to her friends."

"I'm not so sure. They came for a reason. Maybe we'll find out at dinner. Are you going to put them up for the night?"

Mona felt frustrated. "I hope not. They have certainly thrown a wrench into the mix."

"We'll play it by ear. Look, I've got to run and

change. See you in a few minutes." Robert blew Mona a kiss before rushing to his house next door.

Violet said, "If you will excuse me, Miss Mona. I'll see you tomorrow."

"Oh no, you don't. You change your clothes and come right back."

Violet protested, "But my clothes are at Mommy's house." She really didn't want to be around Mona's friends. She admired them, but felt intimidated.

"Borrow an outfit of mine. After all, you've made most of my clothes. I mean it, Violet. I need another woman's support at dinner with these interlopers."

Violet realized Mona felt a little overwhelmed by the surprise visit of these three formidable women and felt glad Mona relied on her. Violet was only too happy to comply. "I'll change into that little brown wool dress I made. It's a bit chilly tonight."

"Wear whatever you want. Just be down here in fifteen. No, make that ten, Violet."

"Yes, Miss Mona," Violet said, scampering off and wondering what shoes and other accessories she would borrow for the dress.

Mona followed her out of the parlor and glanced up the grand staircase. Except for Violet's footsteps up the stairs, it was quiet. Mona went into her office and picked up the phone, dialing. "Phoenix Hotel. Is this reservations? Yes? Good. I'd like to reserve the largest suite you have with three bedrooms. You do? Reserve in the name of Mona Moon. That's right. Mona Moon. How long? Not sure. Let's say for several weeks. I need the room ready tonight. Yes, thank you. Appreciate your understanding. Thank you. Thank you. Good night."

Mona was pleased that the Phoenix Hotel could accommodate her friends. The burning question was—how was she going to get rid of them?

10

"Don't worry about us, dear," Aloha said when Mona explained at dinner that she had booked a suite for them at the Phoenix Hotel. "I've always wanted to explore Mammoth Cave and that's where I intend to visit this week."

Alarmed, Mabel admonished, "I won't have a Floyd Collins incident right before Mona's wedding. You're too much of a daredevil. I won't have it."

"Geez, when did you become my mother, Mabel?" Aloha retorted, angrily.

"Who is Floyd Collins?" Violet asked, looking about the table.

Mona answered, "It happened when you were a little girl. An explorer got stuck in the Mammoth Cave system and died. His name was Floyd

Collins. It was all over the news. Even made the front pages of the New York papers."

"How dreadful," Violet replied.

"Well, I'm going. I'll be back before the wedding." Aloha turned to Mona. "So sorry, my dear, but your little hamlet of Lexington is quaint and charming and also a trifle boring. No nightlife. No nightclubs. No racing except for horses. I need a little more stimulation."

"How would you know, Aloha? You just arrived today," Mabel stated.

"All I had to do was look around the town when we drove through. Two main thoroughfares with local domestic stores. After that, nothing but odorous horse farms and crooked, narrow roads."

"I think you will enjoy Mammoth Cave," Mona said, happy that she was getting rid of one of the ladies. "Besides, I have a million things to do before the wedding. I wouldn't be a good hostess."

"Good. Then I won't be in the way," Aloha said, giving a knowing look at her other two companions. Would they get the hint?

Georgia said, "Well, I'm staying. Mooncrest

Farm seems quiet, and I love the light. I would like to paint here."

Flabbergasted, Mona tried to sway the prickly artist. She hadn't even invited the woman to the wedding and found it unconscionable to be saddled with her. "I'm sure the Phoenix Hotel can accommodate your desire to paint. The suite is ready tonight if you wish to partake."

Robert intervened. "I'm afraid Moon Manor is busy with preparations. You'll find Mooncrest Farm quite noisy and distracting. It is a working farm."

"I don't like noise, but I dislike hotels even more."

Making a last-ditch effort at getting Mona rid of this artist, Robert offered, "There is a cottage at the back of my property. Not much to look at, but it has electricity and running water. It's clean and away from people."

"All I need is an easel and some canvases. I brought my own paint and brushes."

Robert nodded. "Then it's settled, Miss Georgia. You'll stay in my cottage," Robert said, looking over everyone's heads at Mona. He crossed his eyes in jest.

Mona mouthed *thank you.*

Mabel continued arguing with Aloha. "I don't know how you say this town is boring when Mona had a murder taking place right under her nose not even a week ago."

Aloha said, "Don't talk about murder, please. My husband's killer was found not guilty when we all know he killed Walter. The pain of that verdict is very fresh in my mind. How the district attorney lost that open and shut case is beyond me."

Mabel bit her lower lip while the rest of the embarrassed company stared at their napkins folded in their laps. "I'm so sorry, Aloha. Very thoughtless of me."

Aloha said, "Murder is not entertainment, Mabel."

"I'd like to hear about your murder," Georgia said, looking forthwith at Mona.

"The upstairs maid was found strangled behind the mares' barn," Mona replied.

Shocked, but intrigued, Mabel asked, "Any idea who did it?"

Aloha gave Mabel a stern look. "What did I just say, Mabel?"

"None, but the victim's name was Mabelle as well, but spelled it differently," Mona said over Aloha's objections.

Mabel clutched at her throat and gulped hard. "My goodness. How odd, but Mabelle is pronounced differently, isn't it? More of a long A and one lingers on the 'belle.'"

"If it makes you feel more comfortable, Mabel, then yes," Mona replied.

"So the murderer could be walking around on Mooncrest Farm?" Georgia asked, poking fun at Mabel.

"Could even be serving our food," Mona teased as Samuel entered the dining room to collect the dinner plates and serve dessert.

Samuel was startled after noticing the guests were glaring at him and hurried out.

A few minutes later, Mr. Thomas came into the room to serve peach cobbler and peach ice cream. "Eat up folks. Last peaches of the season until next year. Got them several days ago. A frost was coming, so every peach still hanging on a tree was picked. We were lucky to get a last supply."

Georgia waved Mr. Thomas away. "No, thank you."

Dismayed that someone would turn down homemade peach ice cream, Mr. Thomas efficiently served the other guests and then returned to the kitchen where Moon Manor house staff, including several Pinkertons, were eating the rest of the peach cobbler with ice cream as well.

Mona did not like food to go to waste, so Moon Manor staff was free to eat whatever was left from dinner. There was no separate menu for servants. Usually, large manor homes served lesser cuts of meat, porridge, and soups made from leftovers for the staff, but not at Moon Manor. Although there was always a hearty, meaty stew on the stove with soda bread, thick with fresh cream butter for the staff, they basically ate what Mona ate.

Mr. Thomas hoped no one asked for seconds as there wouldn't be any. He barely got the last scoop of cobbler when young Obadiah, a member of the kitchen staff, reached for it. Mr. Thomas slapped Obadiah's hand with a spatula. "Young man, I believe you ate your helping."

Obadiah gave Mr. Thomas a cheesy grin.

His brother, Jedediah, asked, "What are they talking about now, Mr. Thomas?"

"They are discussing Mabelle's murder," Mr. Thomas answered. "Not that it is any of your business."

"Just asking." Obadiah took the last spoonful of ice cream and cobbler from his bowl and licked the spoon.

A knock sounded on the kitchen screen door. Jedediah opened it and a little boy wandered in. His brown eyes widened at the sight of Mr. Thomas' peach dessert on the table.

"What you want, boy?" Jedediah asked, recognizing him as one of the farm worker's sons.

"I have a letter for Miss Mona." He handed Jedediah a sealed envelope and peeked around Jedediah to get a better look at the peach cobbler topped with ice cream heaped in a bowl.

Sighing, Mr. Thomas pushed the dessert away from him. "Son, do you like peaches?"

The boy nodded enthusiastically.

"Here you go then." Mr. Thomas patted the chair next to him and slid the bowl over to the young boy, who dove into the peach dessert with relish.

Jedediah held the envelope up to the light before Mr. Thomas snatched it out of his hand.

"It's for Miss Mona."

"Like I said, it's none of your beeswax." After giving Jedediah a stern look, Mr. Thomas wearily went into the dining room. "Excuse me, Miss Mona, but this just came for you."

11

"Thank you, Mr. Thomas," replied Mona. She recognized the scrawl on the thick envelope—*Need an answer tonight.* It was from Jellybean Martin.

Mona stood and announced, "I'm sorry, but I have to attend to business that can't wait. Violet will accompany you upstairs if you are not going to the Phoenix Hotel tonight. If you need anything, ask her or ring for Mr. Thomas." She beckoned to Robert.

"Thank you for letting us stay the night. I just couldn't go back to town tonight. I'm bushed," Mabel declared. "We'll leave in the morning after breakfast."

"Good night," Aloha said, curious about the envelope.

"Sleep tight," Mabel said while nudging Georgia, who was nodding off. Getting no response, Mabel picked up Georgia's hand to wave goodnight.

Mona and Robert quickly withdrew to her office where they both sat in front of the fireplace.

"What's going on?" Robert asked.

"I went to see Jellybean today. Asked him to search the room of a *Wall Street Journal* reporter."

"How do you know there's a reporter from the Wall Street Journal?"

"Belle told me."

"Ah, the incomparable, all-knowing madam."

Mona took a letter opener and sliced open the envelope. Inside was a two-page workup of an article the reporter was writing.

Robert looked over Mona's shoulder. "What's this?"

"I'm afraid it's an exposé on us, Robert."

"Read it to me, Mona."

"As you wish."

Madeline Mona Moon is currently engaged to Robert Farley, Duke of Brynelleth, and will be married this month. Once again, one of our most beautiful American flowers will be handed over to a penniless British aristocrat. Since the 1880s, Englishmen have haunted our shores in search of wealthy young heiresses. Why? Because after they have run their own estates into penury through gambling, laziness, whoring, and drink, they seek out our American womanhood to save their slothful hides.

Mona Moon, heiress to the Moon estate, has proven herself to be a capable leader. A believer in New Deal principles, Miss Moon has proven again and again that if companies invest in their workers, the return is twofold. She has devoted large sums of money for health care, education, and suitable housing for Moon Enterprises' workers, who are paid higher wages than most of her contemporary business associates. The added wages are then spent by the employees to boost the local economy. Besides more money in the community, the return for the dollar spent is employee loyalty. There has not been any employee unrest in any of Moon Enterprises' companies, which are making profits while putting men back to work.

What has Robert Farley done? By some accounts fleeced Mona Moon of ten thousand pounds to restore his crumbling ancestral home. Here's advice from American men—get a job, Duke of Brynelleth!

Michael Blodgett
The Wall Street Journal

Mona started to rip the papers up when Robert stopped her, grasping the article. He read it carefully.

Tearing up, Mona could see the hurt and shame on Robert's face. "Robert, let me have the article. I'm going to burn it."

"No, you're not. There's nothing in this story that is not true."

"Surely you are not suggesting that we let this Blodgett fellow run the story?"

"Why not?"

"Because it will affect our marriage. Get us off to a bad start. You love me for me. I know that."

"I do love you, but maybe we should think this marriage through again. What am I bringing to the table, Mona? A rundown estate and I am an alcoholic. The money I inherited is in a trust. Can only be used for personal upkeep, medical bills, and education for our children. I can't touch the principal. I'm not a great catch."

"I said I would marry you if you were sober for a year. That year comes to fruition in ten days."

"What if I can't stay sober?"

"We will deal with that if it happens, but I have faith in you, Robert."

"You told me that if I started drinking again, you would leave me. I am weak like other men. What if I can't stay the course? I would be so devastated if you left me that I wouldn't want to live. There will be times that I will stumble. I know I will."

Mona grabbed hold of Robert as he put his arms around her. Burying her face in his chest, Mona smelled cologne, cigarette smoke, and that erotic manly scent that was unique to Robert. "Don't bolt on me now, Lord Bob. It's taken us a long time to get to this point." She looked up at him. "I can live without you and even thrive, but I don't want to. You're my man and I'm your woman. Now we are going to get married soon and that's that."

Anxiety drained from Robert's face. Laughing, he picked Mona up and swung her around before putting her down. "I know who's going to be the boss of this family, and I don't think it will be me."

Mona held out her hand. "How about an equal partnership?"

"I'll agree to that." Robert shook Mona's hand. "Now let me take care of this Michael Blodgett."

"No, all you'll do is punch him in the nose."

"Is that such a bad idea?"

"Oh, I would love it if you did, but it will result in bad press. Let me take care of this. You have your hands full with keeping Georgia O'Keeffe occupied."

"Talk about entitlement. The English have nothing on her. She's formidable."

"Yeah. Keep her out of my way."

"I'm going to stow her in that cottage with food and drink. Hopefully, we won't see much of her. What are we going to do with Mabel?"

"I'll have Jamison drive her and Aloha to the Phoenix tomorrow morning after breakfast. Look, darling, I've got to get back with Jellybean about this exposé tonight."

Robert said, "I should come with you."

"Please take care of the guests. It would be better if I deal with this alone. I don't trust your temper."

"You don't mean alone—alone?"

"I'll take one of the Pinkertons with me. I'll be careful. Promise."

"Call me when you get back. I don't care how late it is."

Mona reached up and bussed Robert on the lips. "I'll be very careful. Don't worry about me. Worry about getting those women out of Moon Manor."

"Will do. See you later."

Robert and Mona left the office together with Robert returning to the dining room and Mona heading out the front door.

It would be a while before they spoke to one another again.

12

Michael Blodgett awoke to the smell of smoke in his room. He sat up and, turning on the nightstand light, was greeted by the sight of Mona Moon lighting his exposé with a match. She let the singed papers flutter to the carpeted floor.

"Who are you?" gasped Blodgett reaching for his glasses, which were of the thick, coke bottle type. As he threw over his covers and struggled to get out of bed, a large man stepped from behind the seated Mona and grabbed him by his pajama collar, wrenching him into a chair in front of her.

Blodgett slapped the man's hand away and tried to recover his dignity by adjusting his pajama top. Smoothing back his limp brown hair with his hands, he asked, "What do you want?"

Looking behind Mona, he noticed another man holding a gun on him.

"You recognize me?"

"Who can mistake that white hair and those yellow eyes? You're Mona Moon."

"Yes, I am."

"You stole my notes and my workup?"

"Mea culpa."

"That's not gonna stop me from submitting it." He pointed to his temple. "I have all the facts up here. I don't need my notes."

"If you insist upon publishing that drivel, Mr. Blodgett, you will be sued for libel. You have your facts wrong."

"How so?"

"I never gave Robert Farley ten thousand pounds. I loaned the Brynelleth estate ten thousand pounds at 1.52 percent interest rate. As for His Grace, Farley was left eighty thousand pounds by his maternal grandmother, which is to care for himself, his wife, and his future children for their lifetimes. So you see he is not impoverished as you suspect."

"Then why doesn't he pay for the restoration of Brynelleth?"

"His Grace's assets are not liquid. He would get nothing back on his return if he dipped into his inheritance. If I do, it is an investment which will be repaid with interest. One would think someone working for the *Wall Street Journal* would understand such loans. In other words, I have invested in the future productivity of a foreign property with reasonable expectation of a return on my investment."

"It still stinks of an English aristocrat taking advantage of American money. That money should stay in the States."

"Think global, Mr. Blodgett. Moon Enterprise will be expanding beyond the U.S. borders if it wants to survive. I see a future where American products will be sold all over the world."

"I thought you were of the leftist bent, Miss Moon? You're sounding like a run-of-the-mill capitalist."

Mona laughed. "I am of the common sense bent. I believe a company can produce a high-quality product and be a good steward of its employees. It should be a win-win situation for everyone. I wake up every morning and wonder if I'm doing right with the money I have inherited.

When I die, I have to answer to God for my actions. You look surprised at that."

"You don't even go to church on a regular basis. I've studied you."

"Church bores me, but I do read my Bible, Mr. Blodgett, and I fear God."

"I don't believe you."

Mona shrugged. "So be it."

"Now what? You gonna have your goons beat me up?"

"Why were you in contact with my maid, Mabelle, the morning of her death?"

"How do you know about that?"

Mona suppressed the urge to gloat. So it *was* this reporter, whom Robert spied talking to Mabelle. "Answer my question, please."

When Blodgett wouldn't answer, Samuel made a menacing move toward him. "Keep that man away from me. I'll have you all arrested for kidnapping and assault."

"If you do, I'll simply purchase the *Wall Street Journal*, have you fired, and then blacklisted from every newspaper in this country."

Blodgett harrumphed. "You don't have the money to buy the *Wall Street Journal*."

Mr. Mott put away his gun. "Laddie, you are out of your depth here. Miss Moon does have the money with lots of pocket change left over. Just tell the lady what she wants so we can go home to our beds. We're not leaving without information."

"Once you get a hold of a man's pants legs, you don't let go." Blodgett hated being bested, but he was alone with three hostile adversaries and his notes had been destroyed, causing him to be at a disadvantage. He made an animal cry, bitterly replying to Mona. "I know when I'm licked. I had been making contact with several of your house staff trying to get the lowdown on you."

"What are you after?"

"Anything that could tie you to corruption or hanky-panky with another man—just something juicy. Mabelle agreed to help me get some pictures of you with Farley in an intimate setting and procure private letters, but she reneged at the last moment."

"With how much money did you bribe her?"

Blodgett looked surprised. "The deal was that I would pay her twenty dollars when she gave me something, but Mabelle told me she felt dirty betraying you and wasn't going to do it."

"You never gave her twenty five-dollar bills?"

"I never pay a source without something in return. Mabelle didn't deliver."

"And you had no further contact with her after your talk in the garden?"

"No. None."

"You didn't threaten Mabelle?"

"No, ma'am, I did not threaten that woman, and I certainly didn't kill her. Reporters don't work that way. We just go on to our next contact."

"How did you gain access to my property?"

"That's easy. I had someone row me to your property via the river. Then I just walked down the farm work roads, acting like I belonged there. No one questioned me."

Mona shot Mr. Mott a menacing glance before demanding of Blodgett, "I want a list of names of those who agreed to help you."

"A reporter never gives up his sources. I won't do it."

Mona leaned in toward him. "I'll make a deal with you. I'll give you a bigger story than me."

"Oh?" Blodgett was intrigued.

"You can chronicle the investigation into Mabelle's murder."

Blodgett affected a yawn. "I'm not a crime reporter. Her murder does not interest me. Business is my beat."

"Would it interest you to know that you are a suspect in her murder?"

Blodgett raised his eyebrows in surprise. "Me? I was here at the time of her death. I have witnesses who can place me."

"Most of the guests who were here that day have checked out and the hotel staff won't remember you."

Blodgett caught the drift of Mona's message and spat out, "I thought Farley was the scallywag, but I see now it is you. You ain't no lady."

Mona replied, "And you are no gentleman, sir."

Mr. Mott tried to reason with Blodgett. "The sheriff could make a good case that you became angry when Mabelle turned you down, and you killed her to exact your revenge."

"I told you that reporters just move on to the next contact."

"And I'm telling you what is going to happen if you don't cooperate, Mr. Blodgett. I will have your guts for garters if you don't cooperate."

"Nice talk from a so-called lady. You kiss Farley with that mouth?"

"Watch what you say, boy," Samuel said, heatedly.

Blodgett glanced at Samuel's massive hands and shuddered. He had been beaten up before by disgruntled men averse to having their lives exposed and didn't want to go through that nastiness again. "Have it your way, but I need something to help my career. Let's make this something we both can live with. Isn't that what you said you try to achieve?"

Mona felt relief. Blodgett was willing to negotiate. She just couldn't have that article published and embarrass Robert. "I will have approval for any wedding article you write about Robert Farley and me for any newspaper."

"Agreed," Blodgett said, sighing.

"After I come back from my honeymoon, I will give you an in-depth interview and you may ask any question about Moon Enterprise business."

Blodgett brightened. "I can ask any question and you will answer?"

"Yes, as long as it is about business. I warn you that I will have witnesses and a stenographer attending the interview, so if you twist anything I say, you will be sued."

"Agreed." He was positively giddy. Mona Moon had never given a newspaper reporter an exclusive interview before. This would put his career on the map.

"I want you to poke around asking questions about Mabelle. If you hear something, even the smallest rumor, contact me. Understand?"

"Agreed."

"You are never to write any article that puts a negative spin on my personal life or Robert Farley. Our personal lives are off-limits."

"Not even fluff pieces?"

Mona thought for a moment. "All pieces must be approved by me. Take the deal or leave it."

Blodgett threw out his hand. "Agreed."

Mona shook his hand and rose from her chair. "We'll now leave you in peace. Good night, Mr. Blodgett." Mona, Samuel, and Mr. Mott left the room with the door closing softly behind them.

Blodgett took a deep breath. Feeling the rapid beats of his heart radically reducing, he lit a cigarette to further calm his nerves. It was a good deal he had struck with Mona Moon, but if push came to shove, he would write what he wanted. Picking up his pocket calendar from the nightstand, Blodgett smiled when he saw there was an appointment tomorrow to meet Mona Moon's aunt—Melanie Moon. He should get some good gossip there. People in town said the two loathed each other. Yep, for sure, he would get a line on some good gossip there.

13

Mona got into the back seat of the car while Mr. Mott and Samuel got into the front. It took a few moments before Jellybean emerged from the shadows and climbed into the back seat with Mona.

"You wanna fill me in?" Jellybean asked Mona.

"He did speak to Mabelle on the morning of her death."

Jellybean reached up in the front seat and poked Samuel in the shoulder. "See, I told you he did it."

"Not so fast, Jellybean. There was another strange man at Moon Manor. Melanie's beau— Enzo Bello. We have two suspects, although I don't see any kind of a motive with either of

96

these men. How would Mabelle's death benefit them?"

Samuel cleared his throat, wanting to ask a delicate question. "Was Mabelle in a state of dishabille?"

Mr. Mott answered, "No, sir. I've seen those types of crimes before, and Mabelle did not suffer that way."

"Our imagination is running away with us." Mona handed Jellybean a wad of five and one dollar bills. "I want Mr. Blodgett watched at all times. Get your friends to help. Here's some money as an incentive for them."

"You want his room searched again?"

"Every day but I think he won't be foolish enough to leave his notes out anymore."

Mr. Mott spoke up, "Our men can watch Blodgett."

"Jellybean's friends are invisible—maids, bellhops, valets, bartenders, waiters, beat cops, just to name a few. Blodgett won't even notice them, but he would a Pinkerton."

Jellybean asked, "Anything else?"

"Did you make contact with Mabelle's cousin?"

"Working on it." He held out his hand and waited.

Amused at Jellybean's hubris, Mona slapped a fifty-dollar bill into his hand. "Thank you, Jellybean, but you better bring me more results or no more fifty-dollar bills for you."

He tucked the bill into his vest pocket. "I'll be in touch." Surveying the street before exiting the black sedan, Jellybean slipped back into the night.

Mona locked the car door. "Let's go home, gentlemen, and get some sleep."

Mr. Mott turned on the car and pulled away from the curb, but not before Enzo Bello stepped out of a dark alley where he had been watching.

Who was that little black man Mona was meeting and what was the man's tie to his future sister-in-law?

14

Several days later, Mr. Mott met Mona in a little cottage at the back of her estate. It was one of the few places Mona could meet with someone and not be overheard, as the Moon Manor staff listened through the heat ducts when they wanted access to information. Even though Mr. Thomas discouraged the practice and Mona had employees sign non-disclosure agreements, the house staff was notoriously nosy. So it was no surprise to Mona that Michael Blodgett had tried to wiggle his way inside Moon Manor—metaphorically, of course.

Mr. Mott did a quick walk about the cottage, making sure no one was lurking about before making his way inside where Mona was waiting for him. "Sorry, I'm late. Had a long meeting with the boys before they started their shifts. What was it you wanted to see me about?"

"Did you get that report on Enzo Bello?"

Mott whistled. "This guy is a real shyster. He's a South American playboy who preys on rich widows. Enzo is a known gambler and horse enthusiast. Apparently, he's very good at polo, which brings him into contact with the swells and attracts the ladies."

"Has he a criminal record?"

"Not that I could find."

"Is Enzo Bello his real name? That is a Spanish name and not Portuguese."

"As far as I can tell. I've telegrammed the American Embassy in Rio for more information. We'll have a fuller dossier in a few days."

"Are you sure he is a Brazilian citizen?"

Mr. Mott shook his head. "Not yet. Like I said, we are still waiting on our contacts in Brazil."

"You say Enzo had no criminal record, but have you pursued any anecdotal stories where he might have been violent toward women?"

"My compadres in Brazil tracked down a story about a woman he was courting who died under mysterious circumstances eight years ago, but no charges were made as the police couldn't prove the death was murder. It was considered suspicious though."

"Was the woman wealthy?"

"No. She was a family friend. The two had grown up together."

"How did the woman die?"

"She fell out of a window three stories up and broke her neck. Apparently, the two had fought that morning and the woman died in the afternoon."

"What did they fight about?"

"The report said neighbors heard them arguing over the fact the woman didn't want to marry Enzo, but they said he left and never returned."

Mona thought of the old adage that some men just don't like being rejected and they object with violence. "Anything else to add about Enzo?"

"Not at this moment, Miss."

"Let me know the moment you receive more information."

"Of course. Is there anything else?"

"Yes, I want to discuss our search of Mabelle's cottage."

"What about it?"

"I've heard through the grapevine that Mabelle had twenty five-dollar bills in her cottage."

"My men found nothing of the sort. What's a maid doing with that kind of money?"

"Whom did you assign to the task?"

"Gunderson and Mason."

"Gunderson. He's new, isn't he? Ginger-haired?" Mona knew Dotty was interested in the recent recruit.

"Yes, but he's a good man. Just came off an assignment guarding the Vanderbilt family."

"Are you sure they didn't find the money? I would like their quarters searched as a precaution."

Mott bristled. "My men are reliable."

"No, they're not, Mr. Mott. Are you forgetting Charlie? He almost caused an international incident and assassinate me in the bargain. I'm sorry, but I don't have the luxury of trusting people, especially men who carry guns. I have people coming onto this estate who shouldn't be here. Security is lax, Mr. Mott. A man, a reporter at that, was able to insert himself onto my property without any notice from your men. A woman was killed within view of Moon Manor. This is unacceptable."

"I know there are gaps in our security. I'm working on correcting our shortcomings."

Mona laughed.

Surprised by her demeanor, Mr. Mott was caught off guard. "What do you want, Miss Mona? My resignation? I'll tender it."

"Mr. Mott, you sometimes amuse me."

"I don't think losing my job during a Depression is amusing and calling my men murderers isn't funny either, Miss Mona. That's what you think, isn't it—that one of us did it?"

Knotting her brows, Mona grew serious. "What I want, Mr. Mott, is that I cancel my contract with the Pinkertons after the murderer is caught. I want my own security team. I no longer want men rotated in from assignments elsewhere. It's like a revolving door. I need men I can trust—local men. Would you be interested in such a position?"

Mr. Mott was taken aback. Wasn't Mona Moon just chastising him? Now she wants him as head of a new security team. He was very confused.

"What about security for the mines?"

"I'll still have the Pinkertons do that for now, but for my own protection, I want men outside the Pinkerton orbit."

"Why me?"

"You're honest and hard-working. You make a good boss. I've not had a single complaint about you. You know how to handle tough men. And best of all—you are not a "yes" man. You tell me what you think."

Mr. Mott blinked. He had a family to worry about. After all, this gig was supposed to have been a temporary assignment, but Mona's offer was tempting. Could he trust her? Mona Moon had always been an enigma to him. But if she was serious, it would mean long term employment in a single locale, and he could relocate his family here.

Mona interrupted his thoughts. "Are all the master keys accounted for?"

"Keys?" echoed Mr. Mott, confused by the sudden change in topics.

"Yes, are all the keys to the estate accounted for? No one is missing a key?"

"No. If any of the men need a key, they have

to go through me. I'm the only one with a key to the lock box where all the masters are kept. Why do you ask?"

"Just asking. We can't afford to have a missing key."

"I'll do another inventory, if you like."

"Please do."

Wanting to return to the part of the conversation where his boss had offered a new position, Mr. Mott said, "Miss Mona, it seems like you're not ready to make a move yet, so why don't we shake hands and pursue this conversation in the future. I would like to explore the possibility."

Mona thrust out her hand.

Mr. Mott shook it.

As she started out the door, Mona said, "Inform me of what you find in those men's rooms."

"Yes, Miss." Mr. Mott followed Mona out of the cottage, but they took different paths. He went straight to the Pinkertons' lodgings, all the while praying he would find nothing untoward in their rooms.

15

What Mr. Mott didn't realize was that late the previous night, Mona and Robert had searched the Pinkertons' office. They found cigar butts hidden under chair cushions, crumpled-up schedules in the wastebaskets, one girlie magazine, and some torn-off paystubs, but no twenty five-dollar bills. Mona gathered all of the tossed paystubs. After doing some calculations, Mona realized the Pinkerton organization was not reimbursing the men close to what she was paying the organization. She found a list of Pinkerton men working at Mooncrest Farm in Mott's locked desk drawer with the amount they were to receive in their checks.

Being a cartographer, Mona was good with math and quickly gauged the monthly amount she sent to the Pinkertons' main office. According to her assessment, the home office was taking too much of an administrative cut and not paying the men their fair share. That left the Pinkerton men with boots in the field vulnerable to bribes and other mischief, which in turn compromised her safety.

Mona felt sorry for Mr. Mott, knowing that she had put him through the wringer. She had deliberately acted odd, trying to throw him off balance, but she needed to know where he stood.

Mona believed that money was like manure. It should be spread around, but she didn't like people taking advantage of her or Moon Enterprises. She was determined to break her contract with the Pinkertons for her personal security, but first she needed to see if Mr. Mott was on the level.

The only thing they had found suspicious was a key taped underneath a filing cabinet drawer. Mona and Robert determined it was a key to the entrance near the gaming room in Moon Manor. Robert had taped the key back, wanting to use it as a trap.

After Mona and Mr. Mott parted, Mona headed for Moon Manor and Robert, who had been hiding in the cottage bedroom, was now following Mr. Mott. She hoped Mr. Mott was searching the Pinkerton's lodgings and not heading back to his office to destroy evidence. Feeling on edge, she had no choice but to wait for Robert's report.

Realizing Mr. Mott's fate rested with Robert, Mona walked through her garden, sniffing the scent of fresh baked pastries. Perhaps Monsieur Bisaillon was making donuts. She decided a cup of coffee and a couple of donuts sounded pretty good at the moment. Mona made her way to the kitchen when she passed the pool and heard a splash.

Startled, Mona glanced over and spied Georgia O'Keeffe taking a dip in her pool—buttnaked! Now Mona was not averse to taking a swim au natural, but tried to be discreet when she indulged herself. Georgia was splashing about and making quite a commotion in broad daylight. Mona looked about for a towel or a robe. There were none. The only things nearby were a pair of well-worn sandals.

Mona was stunned. That meant Georgia had walked from Robert's cottage to Mona's pool in her birthday suit. Mona didn't know whether to laugh or curse at the prickly artist. She walked to the edge of the pool.

Seeing Mona standing by the pool's edge, Georgia stood up in the shallow. Mona had to admire Georgia's bravado. The woman was not the least embarrassed or ashamed of being stark naked.

"Morning," Mona said.

Georgia looked at the sky. "It's going to be a nice day."

Mona followed Georgia's gaze into the sky before returning her attention to the woman. "Just wanted to check that you have everything you need."

"I do," Georgia answered briskly. "Water is getting too cold, though. Don't you have a heater for this pool?"

"It is fall," Mona replied. "Perhaps Robert's pool is warmer. It's more directly in the sun and private."

"I'll try it next time."

"Georgia, I have plenty of swimsuits. Would you like to borrow one? Perhaps a one-piece suit would keep you warmer?"

"No, thank you. My own skin will suffice. Swimming opens my pores."

"I see." Mona bit her lip to keep from chortling.

Just then Mona heard, "Yoo-hoo, Mona."

Mona turned around and saw Wilhelmina Deatherage coming toward her. Oh, no! There was no way to handle this situation other than act as if nothing was untoward.

"Mona, I've been all over the grounds looking for you. We're to go over the guest list for the final time. Dotty's waiting for us."

"Oh, yes, Willie. I forgot about the time. So sorry."

Willie stopped by the edge of the pool and looked down.

Mona watched the color drain from her friend's face as Willie realized that a person was swimming in Mona's pool without the benefit of a bathing outfit. Acting nonchalant, Mona said, "Willie, may I introduce Georgia O'Keeffe. She's a friend of Mabel Dodge."

Rebounding, Willie leaned down and shook Georgia's outstretched hand. "Nice to meet you, Miss O'Keeffe."

"Georgia, this is my good friend, Wilhelmina Deatherage."

Georgia replied, "Nice to meet you as well."

Mona said, "Miss O'Keeffe is a painter."

Willie snapped, "I know who Miss O'Keeffe is, Mona." Addressing Georgia, she continued, "I've seen photographs of you that your husband, Alfred Stieglitz, took. I visited The Intimate Gallery in 1925 for the show your husband organized. Let me think now—it was *Alfred Stieglitz Presents Seven Americans: 159 Paintings and Photographs*. I think I still have a catalog of it."

Georgia gave a whisper of a smile, "It's very kind of you to remember. The show was a critical success, but we didn't sell anything."

"That's not correct. You sold a painting, Miss O'Keeffe. You were the only artist who sold in the show."

Georgia smiled.

Mona couldn't believe it. Georgia smiled. Astonished, Mona glanced at Willie in awe.

"You appreciate art, Miss Deatherage?"

"It's Mrs. but please call me Willie. Everyone does. And yes, I like art very much, but I'm not very knowledgeable about it. I just know what I like."

Georgia climbed out of the pool. "Then you must come to see my new painting today. I've been working on it for several days." She waved her arm to the east. "My cottage is over there. It has the Mexican sunflowers growing in front. Come after you visit with your friend, Mona. I will show it to you."

"I shall and thank you, Miss O'Keeffe," Willie replied, a bit confused as to why Georgia was excluding Mona.

"Call me Georgia," the artist called out over her shoulder as she stepped into her sandals and strolled away.

Willie and Mona watched Georgia disappear behind garden shrubbery until Willie turned to her friend. "Has that woman snapped her cap?"

Mona threw a hand up to her mouth to stifle the giggles. Soon, Willie joined her and they laughed all the way back to Moon Manor—their arms locked at the elbows, wrapped around each other in friendship.

16

"What are you two laughing about?" Dotty asked, entering the library.

Willie explained, "We just had the strangest encounter with Georgia O'Keeffe. She was naked as a jaybird swimming in Mona's pool, and Mona introduces me to her as though nothing was amiss. The woman didn't try to cover up or act the least bit embarrassed. Imagine going naked with all these men working about the farm."

"All artists must be crazy," Dotty replied, handing Mona a telegram. "Speaking of crazy, Jean Harlow said she is coming to the wedding along with William Powell."

Astonished, Mona said, "She wasn't even invited. The nerve of these people inviting themselves."

"Well, she's coming, Mona," Dotty said. "Shall I reserve a suite for her?"

"No, tell her we're full up."

"You better let her come, Mona. If you don't, it will be in all the movie magazines that you slighted Jean Harlow. That's not good publicity since the two of you look like twins," Willie explained.

Mona decided that Willie was correct. She again realized why so many of her business peers and Robert's friends slighted her when they first met. Being aloof was one way to protect oneself from being used. Otherwise, it was a death by a thousand cuts. Ever since the newspapers had printed a picture of her dancing with David Windsor, the Prince of Wales and Heir Apparent to the throne of the United Kingdom, when Mona had visited Robert's ancestral home in England, she had been hounded by charities wanting money and social climbers wrangling to get close. Eleanor Roosevelt had been right— Mona's life was not her own anymore. She had to tread carefully where the public was concerned.

Sighing, Mona ordered, "Dotty, send Miss Harlow a telegram that a suite at the Phoenix

Hotel has been reserved for her the day before the wedding until the day after with my compliments and that she is invited to the reception along with Mr. Powell."

Dotty made a note. "Will do."

"Anything else?"

"Lady Alice sent a telegram stating that she and Ogden will be here at three on Saturday. They will change trains in Cincinnati at eleven that morning."

Mona clapped her hands in glee. "Oh, that's wonderful. I was waiting to hear from Lady Alice about her arrival time. I think Robert and I should meet them in Cincinnati and return with them on the train."

"Why not bring them down in a car?" Willie asked.

"I think a train would be less trouble. US 25 is so narrow and curvy. I always take the train to Cincinnati instead of driving. Besides, it will give the four of us time to visit and decompress."

"Are Lady Alice and Professor Nithercott still staying at Moon Manor?" Dotty asked.

"Yes, Lady Alice is my Matron of Honor."

Dotty announced, "Well, that brings up a

problem with another Alice."

"Uh oh," Willie said, throwing a darting look at Mona.

"Are you referring to Alice Roosevelt Long-worth?" Mona asked, hoping that the answer would be no.

"Here. Read it for yourself." Dotty handed the telegram to Mona, who took it reluctantly.

Mona read it out loud.

"Yours truly will be there for the wedding STOP Why was I not asked to be the Matron of Honor STOP Who is your best friend if not me STOP ARL

"Now I see why you and Robert wanted to elope," Willie commented. "Everyone is pestering you."

"I don't understand why Alice Roosevelt goes on about her father being an attention hog when she's just the same," Dotty said.

"Who's an attention hog?" asked Robert, striding into the room looking flush. Mona noticed the red tint on Robert's face made his features more ruggedly handsome while her platinum hair and amber eyes looked clownish if she blushed. "Alice Roosevelt Longworth, that's who."

"What's Miss Precious up to now?" Robert asked, before sitting down next to Willie and patting her on the knee in greeting.

"Alice Roosevelt is mad because she's not my Matron of Honor."

"She *is* the daughter of a president," Robert replied.

"A dead president," Dotty reminded.

"Make Alice the honored guest at the reception," Robert suggested, grabbing the telegram from Mona's hand and reading it. "That will soothe her ruffled feathers."

"Which Alice?" Mona bemoaned. "Alice Roosevelt or Lady Alice Nithercott?"

"The problem is there are too many *Alices* at this wedding," Willie said. "Tell Alice Roosevelt not to come."

"Yes, please," Violet said, holding the door open for Samuel, who carried a tray of hot coffee and freshly baked cinnamon rolls. "Just came out of the oven. No pun intended." She giggled and then became slighted when no one laughed. "Wow, tough crowd this morning."

"I think it might be more of a double entendre," Dotty offered.

"It was a pun," Violet insisted.

Listening to the friendly banter, Mona immediately forgot her predicament and settled down to enjoy a warm cinnamon bun.

"'Yes, please' to what, Violet?" Robert asked.

"Huh?"

"You said, 'Yes, please.' Referring to what?"

"Tell Alice Roosevelt to buzz off. She always calls me Bucktooth Becky."

"I thought you two had made up when in Washington," Willie said.

"They did," Mona replied. "Violet knows that Alice R is only teasing her."

"I know my teeth need some work, but they are not buck. My left incisor is a little crooked, but other than that, perfectly straight."

"If Alice R didn't like you, she wouldn't tease you. She would just ignore you like you were a piece of furniture," Robert said, before taking a bite of his cinnamon bun and then moaning. "Oh, my goodness. This is a perfectly divine pastry. It almost makes me want to learn how to bake."

"Robert, be serious," Willie chastised.

He nudged her. "I am serious. Take a bite, Willie. Go on. Go on."

Willie bit into the bun and her eyes lit up. "Now I see why you put up with that odious Frenchman. He's a wonder with a bit of flour."

"Excuse me, Mrs. Deatherage," interrupted Samuel, "but Obadiah made the cinnamon buns. Monsieur Bisaillon went to bed with a migraine and refuses to cook today."

"Tell Obadiah that these are the best cinnamon buns I've ever had," Mona said. "That should get Monsieur Bisaillon out of bed."

Reaching for the largest bun on the tray, Dotty said, "I have a feeling that I will be skipping lunch today. I wonder how many calories are in this." She glanced at everyone with a grin. "But I don't care." She took a large bite and, like Robert, almost swooned.

"Obadiah will be pleased to know. Thank you." Samuel poured the coffee and then left the room.

As soon as Samuel vacated, Willie asked, "How old is Obadiah?"

"I can't get a straight answer out of him, but I

think he's no older than seventeen. I think Obadiah lies because he fears I might fire him."

"Why would you do that?" Willie asked.

"Because if he's under eighteen, I want him to finish school. Violet is investigating the matter."

Violet piped up, "Dotty and I are going down to the courthouse to find his birth certificate when we have the time."

Willie asked, "What will you do if you find out that he's younger than eighteen?"

"Make a deal with him and his brother Jedediah like I did with Violet. I want all my staff to have an education. I think that is an American birthright."

Dotty started to say something when Mr. Thomas entered the room. "Excuse me."

"What is it, Mr. Thomas?" Mona asked.

"May I see you, Miss, and His Grace for a moment, please?"

"Of course. Excuse us, please," Mona said to the ladies, reluctantly putting down her pastry and following Mr. Thomas into the gaming room with Robert close behind her.

As they entered the room, Mr. Thomas closed the door, leaving them alone with Sheriff Monahan. Upon seeing the sheriff, Mona rushed toward him. "Have you found Mabelle's murderer?"

A look of discomfort crossed Monahan's face.

"Darling, I think the good sheriff has something to tell us," Robert said. He was curious as to why the sheriff seemed nervous.

Monahan took off his Stetson and held it with one hand on his protruding gut. "I'm afraid I have some questions to ask of the Duke. I asked Mr. Thomas for His Grace alone."

"You may ask in front of me," Mona said. "We have no secrets."

Monahan glanced at Robert, who nodded in agreement.

Robert reassured the sheriff. "It's fine, Sheriff. Ask away."

"Very well, then. There have been some accusations against you, Your Grace." He shifted his weight on another leg.

Robert arched an eyebrow. "What kind of accusations?"

"Did you have a relationship with the deceased woman, Mabelle Taylor, sir?"

"I barely knew the woman's name. The British

are not like the Americans. We take very little notice of servants."

Monahan hid his irritation at Robert's air of superiority. "That's not a denial, Farley."

Mona was a bit miffed herself. She knew Monahan was angry. He had gone from addressing Robert as Your Grace to Sir and now his surname. Not a good sign.

"I knew the woman's name and her position in Moon Manor. Other than saying 'Good morning' or some other pleasantry, we had no exchange."

"Are you sure? I've always understood English lords take advantage of servants, especially when they are young and pretty."

Bristling at the implied insult, Robert replied, "Mabelle was neither. Even if she was, I am engaged to Miss Moon. I would never betray that trust."

"I understand you are a drinking man. In fact, weren't you arrested for being drunk in front of Belle Brezing's place some months ago?"

"You know I was and that it was a setup. I haven't had a drop of liquor in almost a year."

"But you were drunk in front of Belle's place?"

"Maybe. Maybe not. Like I said, I was set up. Talk to the Lexington police."

"What are you getting at, Sheriff? Get to the point," Mona said.

"A witness said you were speaking with Mabelle hours before her death."

"I never spoke to the woman except pleasantries, and I certainly never engaged her on the morning of her death."

"A reporter from the *Wall Street Journal* was here that morning, and he interviewed Mabelle. He wanted her to steal documents. There was also another man here that morning—Enzo Bello. He's engaged to my aunt," Mona offered. "He could have run into Mabelle."

"Who insinuated that I was speaking with Mabelle?" Robert asked.

"Confidential information I'm afraid."

"I know who," Mona said, snapping her fingers. "Sheriff, my aunt was at Moon Manor the morning of Mabelle's death. Her fiancé, Enzo Bello, was with her, like I said. Melanie wanted a joint wedding ceremony with Robert and myself. When I refused, Melanie was miffed. If this eyewitness account comes from Melanie Moon, it is highly suspect. My aunt doesn't like to be told no."

The sheriff flipped his hat while thinking about what Mona had told him. "I see. Just wanted to get a few things straight. That's all. Thank you for your time. I'll see my way out."

"You can go this way, Sheriff." Mona led him to the hallway door.

Sheriff Monahan stopped, looking at the hallway and the door leading outside. "You ever figure why no one saw Mabelle leave Moon Manor?"

Mona replied, "My guess is that she left by this entrance."

"Maybe. Maybe. But Mabelle would have to walk in front of the house in order to get to the barn. The other maid, Dora, would have seen her as she was washing the windows."

Robert said, "Who said Mabelle was killed at the horse barn? Couldn't she just have easily been murdered somewhere else and then placed at the horse barn?"

Monahan asked, "Murdered inside Moon Manor, you mean?"

Mona whispered from the side of her mouth,

"You're not helping, Robert."

"Do you think Mabelle was killed inside Moon Manor, Miss Mona?" Sheriff Monahan asked.

"No, I don't, Sheriff."

"Then one of your staff is lying about seeing her leave. There was you, Mr. Thomas, Dora, Obadiah, Jedediah, Samuel, Dotty, Violet, and Monsieur Bisaillon in this house at the time of her death and no one sees her leave?"

"It's possible," Robert said.

"But not probable," the sheriff countered. "I'm not even mentioning all the Pinkertons and the farm laborers stationed about the farm."

Robert and Mona glanced at each other.

Sheriff Monahan put his Stetson back on and tipped the brim of his hat to Mona. "Something to think about." He gave the couple a sly grin before slipping outside.

Mona closed and locked the door behind him. Suddenly she was not interested in joining the crowd in the library and consuming cinnamon buns. What if Sheriff Monahan was right? Was there a murderer running loose in Moon Manor?

17

Mona pulled the rope in the gaming room for Mr. Thomas. In a few moments, he appeared. "Yes?"

"Would you please send for Dora? I'd like to see her."

"Of course. Do you need anything else?"

"No, thank you, Mr. Thomas."

Mr. Thomas nodded and left the room.

"Why do you want to see Dora?" Robert asked, taking out his cigarette case. Seeing Mona twist her lips in disapproval, Robert took out a cigarette and lit it. "Sorry, my American cow, but this is the only room in the house where I'm allowed to smoke, and I need something to calm my nerves since you won't let me drink."

"What did you discover, Robert?" Mona

asked, waving away the smoke.

Robert took a deep draught and then put out the cigarette. "Mr. Mott did go to Gunderson's and Mason's cottages and search. He found nothing. If those men took money out of Mabelle's home, they have hidden it elsewhere on the premises or spent it."

"Did Mr. Mott check for the key taped under his desk drawer?"

"Mott never went back to his office."

"Why do you think there is an extra key?"

"Maybe in case he has to get into Moon Manor for an emergency—a backup key."

"Where's Mott now?"

"He told his men he was going to the telegraph office in town to see if there were any messages from Brazil about Enzo Bello. Then, he's probably going to check the bars that his men favor and see if they have spent large amounts of five-dollar bills. That's what I would do."

"Can you go into town and perhaps pick up Mr. Mott's trail? I would like to know where he goes."

"I'll see what I can do. Be back for tea, hopefully." Robert reached down and kissed Mona. "Lock the door after me."

She followed him to the side door, let him out, and then locked it.

"You needed to see me, Miss?"

Startled, Mona swung around.

Dora stood with her hands tucked under a white, starched apron several feet from Mona.

"You gave me a fright, Dora. I didn't hear you."

"So sorry, Miss Mona, but I try to be quiet as not to disturb anyone."

"Let's go into the gaming room. I have a few things I would like to ask of you."

"I hope my work is satisfactory, Miss Mona. I work ever so hard."

Mona glanced at Dora's frightened face. "You're not in trouble, Dora. I just need to clarify where everyone was on the morning of Mabelle's death. That's all." Mona waved Dora into the gaming room and took a seat by the window. She held her hand out to the other chair.

"I prefer to stand, Miss."

"I would prefer it if you would sit." Mona could see the throbbing of the vein in Dora's neck. "Please."

Dora sat in the chair. "Thank you, Miss." She pulled her dress over her knees and straightened a spotless apron before giving her attention to Mona.

Mona noticed there was a small run in Dora's wool stockings that was fixed with clear fingernail polish. "I need your help, Dora."

"Me?" Dora asked, looking astonished. "How can I help you?"

"By telling me the truth."

Dora shifted uncomfortably in the chair. "I always tell the truth, and I've never stolen anything. I'm a good girl."

"I know you are a good employee, Dora. I don't want to talk about the quality of your work."

Looking down at her hands folded in her lap, Dora whispered, "It's about Mabelle, isn't it?"

"You have worked in Moon Manor for a long time, haven't you?"

"Yes. Since I was fourteen."

"You worked for my uncle."

"I started as a dishwasher in the kitchen. I kept the kitchen clean. I was moved up to the position of downstairs maid. The pay is higher

129

and a lot less strenuous."

"When did Mabelle start working here?"

"She was here before I was. Mabelle was Miss Melanie's personal maid."

"Mabelle was Aunt Melanie's maid?"

"Yes, for several years."

"She wasn't Miss Melanie's maid when I arrived."

"No, Miss. They had a falling out, and Mabelle became the upstairs maid when the position opened. Mr. Thomas installed her as the upstairs maid. This happened before I came to work at Moon Manor."

"You came to work five years ago."

"Yes, Miss. Your uncle hired me as a favor to my father. He worked on the farm and had an accident. My mother tended to my dad while he recovered, and I went to work to support the family."

"I'm very sorry, Dora."

"It worked out fine. I'm very happy."

"Glad to hear, but I'm confused. Repositioning Mabelle would have been under Mrs. Haggin's purview as she had the final say over female staff," Mona said, speaking of the former housekeeper who had murdered Mona's uncle.

"Mr. Thomas went to Mr. Moon and asked that Mabelle be re-assigned as the upstairs maid."

"Was this over Miss Melanie's objections?"

"Mr. Moon was vexed over his sister's extravagant spending and did as Mr. Thomas asked."

"How did Mrs. Haggin take it?"

"Not very well, as I recall."

"So there was lots of bad blood between Mabelle, Mrs. Haggin, Miss Melanie, Mr. Thomas, and my uncle."

"It was a very tense time. There were grudges all the way around."

"Knowing my aunt—what did Melanie accuse Mabelle of doing?"

"A gold brooch had gone missing."

"Really?"

"Miss Melanie filed for the insurance and after she received the check, the brooch was discovered in the laundry room tangled in some bed sheets. Again, I wasn't working here at that time, Miss Mona. This is what I was told."

"Who told you the story?"

"Miss Melanie's daughter, Meredith. We are about the same age, and we used to look at movie magazines together. She was lonely and so was I. For a time, we were friends."

"I see. Do you think Mabelle took it?"

"I don't know, but she had a weakness for jewelry. All I can tell you is that it was a cheery day for Mabelle when Miss Melanie moved out of Moon Manor and a sad day for me when Miss Meredith left as well."

Mona decided to throw Dora off balance. "How much money did Michael Blodgett offer you, Dora?"

Dora looked up in surprise. "What?"

"Mr. Blodgett has already told me that he contacted Mabelle and was going to pay her twenty dollars to pinch some letters or photographs. Now if he contacted Mabelle, then he must have approached you, too. I want the unvarnished truth."

Dora dabbed her eyes with her apron as tears escaped down her cheek. "I told her not to get involved. I told Mabelle that she was foolish—that she could lose her job and then where would she be. Homeless. Bumming a ride on the railways like the other hobos."

"Mr. Blodgett also told me that Mabelle

turned him down on the morning of her death, so who else did she meet, Dora?"

"I don't know. She said she was meeting Mr. Blodgett and for me to cover for her."

"You saw her leave the house?"

Dora bowed her head in shame. "Yes, she left by the side door and walked in front of the house. I saw her when I was washing the parlor windows. She waved to me."

"To meet whom?"

"Mr. Blodgett."

"No. She met Mr. Blodgett in the garden at the back of the house. She would have had to walk behind the house to meet Mr. Blodgett, meaning she would have turned left. They were seen by His Grace. Who else was she meeting?"

"I don't know!" Dora cried. "I don't. I thought it was this Mr. Blodgett chap and she was going to turn him away, but she never came back. I waited and waited until I became frightened. Where was Mabelle? It wasn't like her to be gone so long, so I ran for Mr. Thomas."

"I think she met Mr. Blodgett earlier in the morning and then met someone else or, at least, bumped into someone."

"I'm sorry I didn't tell everything, but I didn't want to lose my situation. I'm not fired, am I? I can't afford to lose this job."

"No, you're not fired, but if you had been up front, it would have saved me a lot of time and effort."

Dora rose. "May I be excused, Miss Mona? I feel my bowels loosen."

Mona reared back in her chair. "We can't have that, but one more thing, Dora. Do you know anything about twenty five-dollar bills in Mabelle's possession?"

"She pulled it out of her savings. Mabelle wanted a new dress, hat, and stockings for your wedding—the whole works. She was even going to have her hair and nails done. She was so looking forward to it."

Seeing that Dora was frightened, Mona said, "Thank you. You may go."

Dora scurried away as Mona stared out the window. She thought about Mabelle taking money out of her savings so she could attend her wedding in a new frock and hairdo. The woman just wanted to look her best. Mona felt both very touched and saddened that Mabelle would spend hard-earned money to attend her wedding. Still, it wouldn't cost a hundred dollars to do all that. What was the money for?

18

Mona went to Mabelle's little house on Mooncrest Farm and searched the closet. There was no new frock hanging up, no new shoes, new purse or any other female attire that looked recently purchased. She did discover a fresh garter belt and silk stockings still in their boxes in the top drawer of the dresser. There were also some loose sepia-toned photographs.

Dumping the contents of Mabelle's dresser onto her bed, Mona checked underneath every drawer, then pulled the dresser out from the wall and felt behind it. She did the same to Mabelle's vanity, pulling it away from the wall. Nothing. Mona searched behind every picture, even the plaster hanging of da Vinci's *Last Supper*. She pulled out every chair cushion, turned every chair over, and checked every cabinet. She even inspected the toilet.

Frustrated, Mona picked up a chair cushion and put it back in the chair. She would have to clean up the mess she created. As she did so, the floor squeaked. Mona rocked back and forth on it. Some of the floorboards were loose. Mona went into the kitchenette, got a butcher knife, and returned to the loose boards, using the knife to pry them up. After putting the wooden boards aside, Mona looked into the empty space below. It was dark.

When Mona first arrived at Moon Manor, she had all the outdated cottages refurbished with kitchenettes, running water, and modern bathrooms. All the old-fashioned outhouses were torn down and filled in. The original design of the servants' houses was kept intact as they were still sturdy. Mona figured she had another fifteen years before they would have to be torn down and rebuilt.

The staff houses had been built in the last century. The cottages were not constructed on the ground, but stationed on four piles of stacked rocks so the house sat up off the ground. This was done to help air circulate under the cottage and prevent moisture and rot. None of the cottages had insulation and they were heated by potbellied stoves. They all had porches on which people would sleep during the worst of the summer heat.

So when Mona peered into the dark hole, she was staring at the ground underneath her—a place where spiders and snakes liked to congregate. Cursing that she did not have the foresight to bring a flashlight, Mona gritted her teeth, closed her eyes, and leaned into the open hole, thrusting her arm into the darkness below. Mona squealed when her hand enclosed on a small, hard object. Bringing it up, she threw it away from her, having it hit against a wall.

Mona checked her arm and hair for spiders. Standing up, she checked her clothes. Oh, she must look a mess. Satisfied that nothing creepy crawly was on her person, Mona glanced at the item she had brought up from its hidey-hole.

It was a small wooden box held together by a dirty string. Mona pulled at the string, which fell apart without much coaxing. Placing the box on a table, she lifted the lid with the knife and peered into the box.

In it was a bank book, crisp five-dollar bills, and a gold brooch.

19

Mona checked the bank book. It was from Mona's bank for the total amount of two hundred and forty-three dollars. What was most important was the book recorded every transaction Mabelle made with Mona's bank. Each time Mabelle deposited or withdrew money, she had to present the bank book so the teller could document the transaction, date, and balance. Mabelle had not withdrawn any money for the past six months. Her last withdrawal was only for thirty-five dollars. Overall, Mabelle was a steady saver.

So that did not address the presence of seventeen five-dollar bills—a total of eighty-five dollars. Mona knew that Mabelle's money hadn't been stolen. It was likely Mabelle was hedging her bets. Lots of people didn't trust banks since many had folded in 1932. The mystery could be that Mabelle stashed money away in her secret hiding place for a rainy day.

Mona hurried to clean up the mess, which took her twenty minutes to put everything back to right including the floorboards. Taking the box, Mona hastened to Moon Manor where she entered through the kitchen.

Monsieur Bisaillon was laying out boards and dowels for Mona's wedding cake and studying how to assemble the seven-tiered white cake with buttercream frosting outside with raspberry mousse between each layer. He had never created so large a wedding cake and wanted to make sure the assembly went smoothly as his reputation was on the line. This was one of many cakes and pastries he would have to prepare for the festivities. There was the pre-wedding party for the Mooncrest Farm and Moon Enterprise's staff, a special tea for VIPs and their wives, the wedding reception and a wedding breakfast the next day plus regular meals for Mona's house guests during the week before the event.

Obadiah was greasing the baking pans for the

cake when Mona entered the kitchen. He stopped what he was doing and wiped his hands on his apron. "Can I help you, Miss Mona?" he asked after he saw that Monsieur Bisaillon was preoccupied with a cookbook.

"I would like to see Mr. Thomas if he isn't busy."

"He's in the butler's pantry."

"Thank you." Mona marched into the butler's pantry and caught Mr. Thomas and Samuel doing inventory of the silver and fine bone china. "You think someone is going to steal our silver, Mr. Thomas?"

"If your future brother-in-law is coming to the wedding, then yes, we do," Samuel said. "I caught him filching a silver candy dish in his pocket. That dish was a gift to your uncle by an early admirer. It's engraved—'Sweets for the sweet.'"

"Oh, my, I didn't know that. I never knew Uncle Manfred had a sweetheart."

"I was a boy, but I remember her."

"Who was she?" Mona asked, inquisitively.

Mr. Thomas interrupted, saying in a low but firm tone, "Quit gossiping and get back to work, Samuel."

"Yes, sir." Chastised, Samuel went back to counting the fish forks.

Obviously, tales of Uncle Manfred's love life were off limits to Mona. Wanting to diffuse the situation, Mona said, "Thank you, Samuel, for retrieving the candy dish. I apologize for my indiscreet comments."

Mr. Thomas nodded and straightened his shoulders, asking, "Might I help you with something, Miss Mona?"

"I see that you are very busy, but may I have a few moments of your time? I want to ask something."

"Very well. Let's step into my office."

Mona followed Mr. Thomas down a short corridor to his office. On his desk were piles of invoices for the wedding lying on top of Mona's checkbook. Mr. Thomas prepared the checks for the household bills while Dotty dealt with the farm invoices, but Mona had to sign all checks with the receipts attached by paper clips. Looked like Mr. Thomas had spent the morning going through the invoices. She sat down while Mr. Thomas rested in a chair behind his desk. "What may I do for you, Miss Mona?"

Mona held up the box, opened it, and lifted out the gold brooch, she handed it to Mr. Thomas. "Do you recognize this brooch?"

Mr. Thomas looked the brooch over and studied it before handing it back.

"Well?" Mona asked.

Mr. Thomas seemed deep in thought with his brow furrowing and his fingers tapping on his wooden desk. He looked like a man who had tasted something overly ripe and on the hairsbreadth of spoiling.

"Mr. Thomas?"

"It appears to be a brooch I saw many years ago. It was lost."

"I thought it had been recovered. Dora told me that it was found in the laundry room, tangled in some sheets. Melanie thought Mabelle had stolen the brooch and had her dismissed as her personal maid. Then you had Mabelle reinstated as the upstairs maid."

Mr. Thomas gave a ghost of a smile. "Caused quite a fuss as I remember."

"Why did you do it?"

"I knew Mabelle never stole this brooch. It was another scheme of Melanie Moon to get her hands on some money." He got up and closed the office door. "This stays between us, but I have never liked your aunt. Even as a young girl, there was darkness within her. She's weak, impulsive, and greedy. Terrible traits in a person who is intelligent, and don't forget that for one moment. Melanie Moon is cunning."

"I thought we weren't supposed to gossip, Mr. Thomas."

"This isn't gossip. It's a fact. I've worked here all my life. Was born on this farm. My family were slaves for the original owners—the Taylors. So were Mabelle, Jamison, Samuel, Obadiah and Jedediah, and Burl's families."

"Wait a moment. Mabelle's ancestors were slaves on this farm? She never told me."

"Her great great-grandmother. Should I say more? You know how it was back then."

"I had no inkling."

"Mabelle kept her background to herself, but never denied it. It was nobody's business as far as she was concerned, so Mabelle didn't elaborate."

"Who did know?"

"Well, anyone in our community would know, but they wouldn't tell any white person. There's white man's business and black man's business. The two don't intertwine." Mr. Thomas gave Mona a faded smile.

"I understand. I've been all around the world and prejudice is alive and well. You don't have to justify Mabelle's background to me," Mona replied. "Do you think Dora knew?"

"I can't see Mabelle telling Dora about her family's past."

"Why did your families stay on the farm?"

"Not all of us did. After the Great War, many went up north to find factory jobs. Some moved to Lexington. Our six families stayed when the Moon family bought the land. They promised to improve our lot in life if we stayed. They needed the support. The Moons kept their word, and we helped build this estate into what it is today. The Moon family has always been good to us, but, Lordy, they were appalling to each other. We saw them boot your father out because he fell in love with the gardener's daughter. You couldn't find a sweeter woman than your mother, but she was not from their class, so the Moon family despised her. Giving you control of Moon Enterprises and Mooncrest Farm was your uncle's way of asking for forgiveness, but as long as your Aunt Melanie draws a breath of life, she will continue to challenge you. It's in her nature. She takes after her father and mother."

Mona held up the brooch. "Mr. Thomas, what is the real story behind this piece of jewelry?"

"It was given by the patriarch of the original family who owned this land. Old man Taylor gave his wife's gold brooch to Mabelle's great great-grandmother to keep her quiet about his son's dalliances with her. I don't know why he just didn't give the woman her freedom, or land, or even a mule. What's a slave gonna do with a gold brooch? She couldn't wear it or even show folks unless she wanted trouble, but it was handed down to the oldest daughter of each generation for safe keeping, but they wouldn't dare wear it."

Mona held up her hand. "Whoa. Whoa. I'm very confused. The brooch was Mabelle's?"

Mr. Thomas nodded.

"Then what's this story about Mabelle stealing from Melanie? Dora said it was Melanie's brooch and accused Mabelle of stealing it."

"Mabelle made the mistake of showing it to

147

Miss Melanie one day, and Melanie didn't believe the story of how the brooch came to be in Mabelle's family. She just decided to steal it, not thinking a servant would make a fuss over its loss, but Mabelle did. That's when Melanie fired her."

"So there was no insurance claim?"

"It's a story your aunt cooked up to cover her tracks. She thought Mabelle would not be able to prove the brooch was hers, but Mabelle produced an old photograph of her mother holding it and showed it to your uncle. He retrieved the brooch from Miss Melanie and made Mabelle the upstairs maid giving her a raise to boot. Your Aunt Melanie was fit to be tied. She couldn't believe a maid had bested her."

"Why not confront Melanie and tell the world the truth?"

"If the story got out that Melanie Moon tried to steal a gold heirloom from a poor maid, she would have denied it and made Mabelle's life a misery in retaliation. Who was going to believe Mabelle?"

The yarn was hard to take in. Mona had been going about solving Mabelle's murder from the wrong end. Could this have been a simple case of robbery gone bad, and it had nothing to do with her or Robert? Mona held out the box to Mr. Thomas. "Know anything about this money?"

Mr. Thomas shook his head. "Naw. Mabelle could have been holding it for someone."

"Like a distant cousin?"

"Maybe. Why don't you ask him?"

"I think I will, Mr. Thomas. Thank you." Disconcerted, Mona left Mr. Thomas' office wondering what other secrets he held concerning Moon Manor.

20

Jellybean leaned up against a makeshift bar in a ramshackle juke joint and ordered a beer.

A large man, wearing overalls over a striped frayed shirt, was playing poker. Noticing Jellybean, he cashed out. "Sorry, boys. Got to see a man about a horse." Picking up three one-dollar bills from the table, he stuck them in his breast pocket before lumbering over across a smoky, dimly lit room. He leaned on the bar next to Jellybean and said in a low voice, "I hear you've been looking for me, my man."

The bartender came over.

The man thumbed at Jellybean. "I'll have a beer and put it on my *friend's* tab."

The bartender glanced at Jellybean, who nodded slightly.

As the bartender poured the beer, the man asked, "Well, what do you want? Speak up or I'm going back to the game."

"Not so loud." Jellybean looked about to see if anyone was listening. "I've got some people who wish to speak with you."

The man glared suspiciously at Jellybean. "Oh, yeah. Who?"

The bartender slapped down a beer in front of Jellybean's *friend*. "That's seventy-five cents for both."

Jellybean threw down a crumpled dollar. "That's an awfully high price for watered-down beer. Mine didn't even have a proper foam."

The bartender sniffled. "Take it or leave it. Makes no never-mind to me."

"Keep the change, brother. Seems you need it more if you aim to cheat a neighbor over a lousy glass of hops."

"You ain't no neighbor of mine," the bartender snarled, wiping up spilled alcohol.

"Prohibition is over or don't you get the news in these here backwoods? No need for home brew anymore," Jellybean mocked.

The bartender made a hissing noise and went

to wait on another customer.

Jellybean took a sip and wiped his face before complaining to the man in the overalls, "It ain't even cold. Aw well, follow me."

"Why should I? Follow you where?"

"Because you want to make some scratch, that's why. Now come on."

The man in the overalls followed Jellybean outside to the back of the juke joint where people were milling about, smoking, or drinking moonshine out of glass mason jars.

Jamison pulled up in an old Model T allowing Jellybean and his compatriot to climb inside. They swung out onto US 25 for a few miles and then made a fast left down a dirt road by the river where a group of hobos sat around a fire roasting hot dogs.

"You stay in the car," Jellybean ordered the man. "We'll be over there."

Jellybean and Jamison climbed out of the car and went over to the fire. To introduce themselves, they pulled out pints of whiskey from their coats and handed the bottles around. One of the hobos gave them hot dogs speared on green twigs. The two interlopers roasted the hot dogs while keeping an eye on the car and jawing with the out-of-work men, hoping to pick up bits of news.

The man in the overalls decided to join them, but as he opened the door, a man entered the car from the other side.

"If you join them, you won't get paid."

"Who are you?" asked the man in the overalls, shutting the car door.

"My name is Robert Farley. Your name?"

The man drew back, suspicious. "Whatcha want with me?"

"I am taking care of Mabelle Taylor's business. I believe she is a relative of yours."

"Might be."

"Look, old chap. I'm not here to shake you down or cause harm. I simply want information, and I would like to know whom I'm dealing with. Now what is your name?"

"Virgil Taylor."

"And you were Mabelle Taylor's distant cousin?"

"Just us two left. Everyone else is dead."

"That explains why you are down here looking for answers to her death."

"Whatcha mean?"

"Well, you are wearing a frayed shirt and overalls that are too big for your build, which means you borrowed them. Your nails are clean and look professionally manicured, even though your hands look rough. Also, your hair has been trimmed and you have recently shaved. I smell your aftershave lotion. You are remarkably well-groomed for being a sharecropper, Mr. Taylor. Men who work the land are less fussy about their appearance."

Virgil Taylor sighed. "I heard there was a man who knew something about Mabelle and he frequented the juke joint. If I came as myself, the man would have bled me dry."

"Why is that?"

"I sell used cars. I buy second-hand cars, fix them up, and then take them to Cincinnati or Knoxville to sell. I make a good living by cutting out the middle man. I don't like grease under my nails. Doesn't look good to prospective customers when I try to sell the cars, so I go to the barbershop once a week." He paused, studying Robert's face. "I'm a very good mechanic."

"What was your plan?"

"I was hoping to find the man, get him drunk, and knock the truth out of him."

"What truth might this man have?"

"I don't know. Just heard a rumor."

Robert was growing impatient. "Look, we are after the same thing—to find Mabelle's murderer. Let's work together."

Virgil said, "I heard that Mabelle's old man might be back in town. He's my prime suspect."

"Mabelle was married? This is the first I have heard of it."

"She got married young, had a baby who died from crib death, and the husband deserted her, leaving town with another woman. Mabelle hadn't seen him for years, but I heard he popped up after her death. Probably after her estate as meager as it was."

Robert suddenly felt ashamed. He had never taken notice of Mabelle, a woman whose life was full of sorrow. "Have you seen this man?"

"No."

"Was she seeing someone? We heard there might be a beau?"

"The last thing Mabelle wanted was to get hitched again. No, the only family she had was me."

ABIGAIL KEAM

"So now what?"

"I'll claim Mabelle's things. I'm her rightful heir. Besides, she was holding money for me."

Perking up at the mention of money, Robert asked, "Money?"

"Mabelle was holding money from a car sale I did in Mt. Sterling."

"Why was she holding the money for you?"

"She always held money for me." Virgil looked sheepish. "I like to play the ponies, so Mabelle hid my money until the itch subsided. Otherwise, I'd be broke."

Robert looked sideways at Virgil. "Perhaps you killed Mabelle because she wouldn't give you back the money?"

Virgil gave a lopsided grin. "There it is. There it is." He wagged a finger in front of Robert's face. "I knew we'd come to this. Sorry to disappoint you, but I was in Cincinnati on the day of her murder. All day. I can prove it without a doubt and have already done so with Sheriff Monahan."

"Sorry, mate, but I've got to look at all possibilities. Besides, I think you are lying."

"Why do you care? Mabelle was a nobody to you."

"That's quite true, but she was somebody to my fiancée."

"Mona Moon. Mabelle talked to me about her. Said Moon was a good employer, and she enjoyed working for her. The woman treated my cousin right."

"Do you know of a Michael Blodgett?"

"No, should I?"

"What about an Enzo Bello?"

Virgil shook his head.

"Did Mabelle talk about any other man? Anyone she had friction with?"

"She complained about Monsieur Bisaillon. She hated that he tuned in Father Coughlin on the radio, and she would have to listen to that prejudiced bastard when she took her breaks in the kitchen. He was always going on about Jew this. Jew that. Mabelle thought it was disgusting."

"Did she and Monsieur Bisaillon fight about it?"

"Yeah. There were words spoken."

Robert took in what Virgil told him. Finally, he asked, "Anything else?"

"I've come up with blanks." He leaned forward in his seat. "Look, Mabelle was holding a hundred dollars for me—all five-dollar bills. I need that money. My rent is due."

"We found eight-five dollars in five-dollar bills, but I don't have it on me. Come to Moon Manor. I know that Miss Mona would like to meet a member of Mabelle's family. We'll have Mabelle's things boxed up for you."

"What happened to the other fifteen dollars?'

"We don't know. A new garter belt and stockings were discovered."

"That's not fifteen bucks."

"That's all we found, Mr. Taylor."

"I'll need gas money."

Robert reached in his pocket and peeled off a twenty-dollar bill. "This should tide you over. Also, I expect you to contact Jellybean Martin if you hear anything else. There will be a small reward in it for you."

"This twenty will go a long way until I get the rest of my money, but you don't need to pay me for information. I want Mabelle's killer as much as you."

"Very well, then. I'll leave you to it. Jamison will drive you back to the juke joint. Goodbye, Mr. Taylor." Robert got out of the car and waved to Jellybean and Jamison.

The two men joined Robert and listened quietly to his instructions. Then the three men split up as Robert disappeared into the woods and Jamison drove off with Virgil Taylor in the back of the car. Jellybean returned to the little group of hobos and listened quietly throughout the night, hoping to discover a nugget of useful information.

He didn't.

21

Robert let himself in with a latch key and took off his shoes before tiptoeing his way upstairs to Mona's room. It was after midnight, and Samuel would be in bed in the staff quarters behind the kitchen while the rest of the employees would be sleeping at their cottages. He didn't know if Violet stayed over in her room off Mona's suite, however, she was a deep sleeper. He knocked softly on Mona's door.

Mona opened the door and let him in.

Chloe was standing on the bed, wagging her tail. She barked a few times.

"Quiet," Robert said, going over and petting the excited dog. "You'll wake the house, Chloe. Now hush." He pulled the dog to him and gave her a hug, which calmed the poodle down. Once calm, Robert put the dog on the floor.

Mona locked the bedroom door. "What news?"

Robert sat on the bed. "Violet here?"

Mona replied, "She went to stay with her mother."

"Good. I need to take a shower, and don't want to run into her."

"Take it over at your own house."

"I'm not leaving. I'm staying close to you tonight. From now on, I want Violet to stay with you and a Pinkerton man stationed in the house. Until I came, there was only Samuel here."

"There's Dora."

"What use is Dora in an emergency?"

Mona shrugged. "I see your point. I'll have several Pinkertons staying in the staff bedrooms until we go on our honeymoon."

Robert seemed relieved.

"Now, what did you find out?"

"I met this cousin of Mabelle's and he lied to me. Fed me the worst rot of bull about the money and his relationship to Mabelle."

"What makes you think so, Robert?"

"Because Mona, my dear, I know men. I

know when they are lying. I think he was Mabelle's boyfriend and didn't want me to know."

"But they were cousins."

"Distant cousins. Remember the current President and First Lady are distant cousins." He pulled Mona to him. "I don't want to talk about him right now. I have other things on my mind," Robert said, nuzzling Mona's neck.

Chloe jumped back on the bed and squeezed in between them, licking both their faces.

"Blasted pooch!" Robert wiped the slime off his face.

"Don't, Robert. You'll hurt Chloe's feelings. Go take your shower and then sleep in Violet's room. It's only a week to our wedding. Let's show a little restraint."

"Come on, lassie girl. Don't make me," Robert pleaded.

Mona pointed toward the bathroom. "March. You smell like campfire smoke."

Robert dragged himself to the shower, complaining all the while. He didn't see Mona grin at his grumbling, nor did Robert realize how grateful she was that he was sleeping in the next room.

Mona didn't tell Robert, but she had caught someone peering in a window while she and Samuel were locking up for the night. Or that someone threw a rock against the house. She would tell him tomorrow morning. Mona laid her pistol on the nightstand, closed the drapes, and checked the door again. It was locked. Climbing into bed, she listened to Robert whistling in the shower. His voice was reassuring as was the presence of her poodle. She lifted the covers for Chloe and gave the dog a kiss on the nose. "Go to sleep now, Chloe."

The dog turned three times before curling up next to Mona and settling in. Taking a deep breath, Mona wished she could be as relaxed as her dog. Maybe if Morpheus granted her wish, she might catch some winks, but she doubted it.

It was going to be a long night.

And it was.

22

Mona pleaded, "Robert, calm down, please."

"The one thing a man ought to do is protect his wife-to-be. I leave one night and some riffraff gets on Mooncrest Farm, throws rocks at the house, and peeps in the windows. Where were your men, Mr. Mott? Where were they?" Robert raved.

Mr. Mott squared his shoulders and looked straight at Robert. "I take full responsibility."

"I don't care if you take responsibility. A woman was murdered on this property right under your nose. Last night another incident—a Peeping Tom. In a few days, this estate will be hosting parties to some of the most important people in the country. I can say that I do not trust Mooncrest Farm security. I don't trust the

Pinkertons to keep everyone safe."

Silence fell upon the room where Mona, Robert, Mr. Mott, Samuel, and Mr. Thomas stood in a circle.

Mona grabbed Robert's hand and squeezed. She thought him right to be so concerned, but Robert's anger didn't solve the problem of lax security. "We have only days before guests start to arrive. Any suggestions?"

"Did you recognize the man in the window?" Mr. Mott asked.

"He was wearing a bandanna pulled over his lower face and a hat. Samuel ran after him, but lost him in the dark. Then about an hour later, we heard a thud against the house. Samuel checked and found a rock had been thrown against the house. We assumed it was the same person," Mona answered.

"Sounds like the person was familiar with the house and knew that we were short-staffed last night," Samuel offered.

"There is a lot of talk in town about this wedding," Mr. Thomas said. "Most people are excited, but there are some who are resentful."

"Which is why we can't have this security

lapse," Robert huffed, feeling his heart race. Mona was right. Yelling was not helping the situation.

Mr. Mott explained, "More Pinkertons will be arriving tonight to pick up the slack. We will have round-the-clock surveillance of Moon Manor and will have sentries stationed by every entrance to the farm and the house. I have already hand-picked squads to guard Miss Moon and her guests. We will be as unobtrusive as possible."

Mr. Thomas cleared his throat.

"Yes, Mr. Thomas?" Mona asked. "You wish to add something?"

"The one thing we are not discussing is food security."

Mona's heart sank. She hadn't even thought about someone tampering with the victuals. "Thank you for bringing that issue up. Have you any suggestions?"

"Locks should be put on all the cabinets, food storage areas, refrigerators, freezers, and animal feed storage sheds after an inventory of food-stuffs is completed. Only Monsieur Bisaillon and myself should have the keys to these areas. One thing I am concerned about are the chickens. The kitchen staff will be using a lot of eggs this week, and we should consider the chickens a high priority. I would hate to see their feed tainted."

"I'll leave it to you to make this happen," Mona ordered.

"May I finish?"

"Please do."

"All the house staff should move back into Moon Manor until you and His Grace leave for your honeymoon."

"Do we have the room?" Mona asked.

"The kitchen staff will sleep in the staff quarters. Violet will stay in her old room upstairs. Dotty can take the last room on the left while Lady Alice and His Grace take the rooms on either side of your suite."

Mona blinked. "You want Robert to stay in Moon Manor before the wedding?"

"I think all hands should be on deck, Miss Mona. Plus the downstairs lights should be kept on all night with all additional outside lighting plus pitch torches stationed about Moon Manor and the driveway. We need more light after dark."

Mona lowered her head in defeat. The security restrictions were daunting. She had wanted the week before the wedding to be enjoyable for her guests and staff. Now instead of just being busy, the staff would be on edge until Mona and Robert were on a train for their honeymoon. She was sure the staff would be glad to see the back of them. "Can we do as you ask without the guests noticing all the precautions?"

Mr. Thomas nodded. "I know the household staff is well trained. None of the guests will notice anything amiss."

"What about our visitor in His Grace's cottage?"

"I have a man shadowing the woman for her protection. She will never know that he is watching," Mr. Mott confirmed.

Robert gave a short guffaw. He was not so sure as he had lost all confidence in the Pinkertons.

Mona remarked dryly, "I'm sure he'll see more than he bargained for." She turned to Robert. "Can you visit Georgia O'Keeffe and see if she is ready to join the other guests at the Phoenix Hotel? Tell her we need the cottage for your Aunt Tilly or someone. She's putting an additional strain on our resources. Now we have to spare a man to watch O'Keeffe for her own protection. You'd think she might be frightened to stay here with a murder unsolved."

Robert shook his head. "That woman fears nothing. Do you know she swims naked in my pool?"

"No, really? Shocking," Mona replied, sarcastically. "All right. I'll tell Miss O'Keeffe it is time to move on." She addressed Mr. Mott. "What about the security at the Phoenix?"

"They have their own house detectives, but we will station a couple of our men in the lobby as well. Also, the Lexington police force as well as those in the surrounding counties have been notified and given the guest list. They'll be on alert for any mischief."

Mona realized the situation had gotten out of hand. Because of Mabelle's murder, she had to double her security and, instead of enjoying the prospect of being a bride, Mona worried about the safety of those attending the wedding. She just wanted to cry.

"Miss Mona. If you don't get a move on, you'll miss the train," Mr. Thomas cautioned.

Both Mona and Robert glanced at their wristwatches.

Mona said, "Oh, gosh, look at the time. We must hurry, Robert."

"By the time you get back with Lady Alice and Professor Nithercott, we will have everything in place. Skedaddle now," Mr. Thomas said.

Mona looked beseechingly at Mr. Thomas. "You promise?"

"Cross my heart."

Mona felt better.

Samuel added, "Don't worry, Miss Mona. We won't let you down."

Robert took Mona's hand. "Let's hurry, darling."

Samuel rushed to gather Mona's hat, purse, and gloves. Robert grabbed his walking stick, overcoat, and hat, meeting Mona at the front door.

Taking Robert's arm, Mona gratefully let him escort her to the car where Jamison waited. Behind her car was another vehicle filled with Pinkertons. The sight of them made Mona's stomach lurch, but she realized guards infiltrating all aspects of her life were her existence now.

She had to get used to it.

23

"Alice! Alice!" Mona cried, seeing her friend step off the train with her husband, Ogden Nithercott at Cincinnati's Union Station.

Upon hearing her name, Alice looked over and spied Mona. Her face lit up at the sight of Mona and Robert rushing toward them. She tugged on Ogden's sleeve and pointed to their friends. Ogden, thrilled to see them as well, dropped his luggage tickets, which he had been trying to hand to the porter. Both the porter and Ogden stooped to pick up the tickets, fluttering in the breezes stirred up by hurrying passengers.

Robert came to their rescue, plucking three flapping pieces of paper from the platform and giving them to the porter along with a five-dollar bill. "Please bring the trunks to Track 31 going to

Lexington. We'll be waiting in the café. Can you bring the new luggage tickets to us?"

"Yes, sir. The Lexington train is already in. It leaves in thirty-five minutes. You'll be able to board in ten." The porter tipped the bill of his cap and went immediately to the luggage compartment, happy that he had obtained such a large tip. His wife wasn't feeling well, so he would take her out for a spaghetti dinner. They might even splurge on the house wine. That would perk his wife up.

"Thank you, old chap. I am all thumbs these days," Ogden said, shaking Robert's hand.

Ogden's grip felt weak to Robert, who narrowed his eyes in concern. "Trouble, Ogden?"

"Old war injury." He whispered, "Let's not talk about it in front of the ladies."

Robert turned to Alice. "Can it be possible that you are prettier each time I see you, Alice? Marriage with this old water buffalo agrees with you."

Blushing, Alice swatted Robert playfully on his chest. Alice had grown up with Robert and his family. They had even been engaged to each other at one time, but Robert's addiction to drugs and alcohol after serving in the Great War had driven them apart. Though they loved each other, they weren't right as marriage partners. No one was happier than Alice when Robert met Mona. Though bittersweet to lose her first love to another, Alice soon met Robert's great friend, Ogden Nithercott and realized that Ogden may not be her first love, but was her great love. Everything had worked out for the best.

Robert grabbed Alice, giving her a proper bear hug.

Mona glanced at Ogden in astonishment. "I thought hugs were very un-English." She had never seen Robert act so warm-hearted.

"I'm so happy to see you both, I could hug anyone," Robert said. "Come here, Ogden. Let me give you a good old-fashion American hug."

Grinning, Ogden sidestepped Robert. "Get a grip on yourself, laddie."

"Uh, oh. Trouble in paradise?" Alice asked, straightening her hat after Robert had crushed it with his embrace. "Robert seems unusually enthusiastic."

Mona placed her hand on Alice's arm. "There's been a murder at Moon Manor. We are on edge and glad to see you both. You have no idea."

"I swear, Mona. You have the most peculiar habit of acquiring dead bodies."

"If you would like to stay at the hotel, instead of Moon Manor, I certainly understand."

"And miss all of the excitement? Not on your life." Realizing what she had uttered, Alice put a hand up to her mouth, giggling, "That came out wrong."

"It's your funeral then, if you stay at Moon Manor," Mona added. Both women chuckled.

"If I feel like death warmed over, I can always relocate to the hotel," teased Lady Alice.

"Righto," Robert said, spotting Michael Blodgett hiding behind a large column with a man who was obviously a photographer. "Let's board the train."

"Yes, let's do. I'd kill for a cup of tea," Ogden said, joining in the game.

"Yes, I see that you are fading fast, Ogden, but before you become food for the worms, let's get on board."

"Blimey, Robert. You just said we should wait in the café for our luggage tickets," Ogden said.

"That was before I spotted our picture being taken. Three o'clock."

Mona, Lady Alice, and Ogden turned to see a photographer snap their picture.

"A friend of yours?" Lady Alice asked wryly.

"How did that nosy reporter know we were on the train?" Robert asked.

Mona explained, "That, my friends, is Michael Blodgett. He's a reporter for a newspaper. I thought we had made a deal, but obviously not. Let's do as Robert asked. We're in a public place and can't control that man's actions."

"You all go to the train. I will hunt down our porter for the luggage tickets," Robert suggested.

Mona and her friends gave a last glance at the reporter and hurried down the main tunnel to their train platform. Settled in their compartment, Mona confessed to the recent events at Moon Manor, telling all to her spellbound guests.

"Oh, we shouldn't have teased about death," Lady Alice said. "All this right before your wedding, too."

"I feel better now that you are with me, Alice."

Lady Alice smiled warmly. She loved Mona

dearly and was happy to help any way she could.

"Look. The train is getting ready to leave," Ogden said, looking out the window. Mona stood and peered out the window as well. All three were concerned with the whereabouts of Robert.

The compartment door was thrown open and Robert entered, grinning. "Here you go, Mona. A little gift from Michael Blodgett." He handed Mona a strip of exposed film.

"How did you get this?" Mona asked, holding the film up to the light.

"I didn't. Your Pinkerton boys did it for me and Mr. Blodgett will not be boarding this train, so we are free to go to the dining car and have a drink in peace."

"There were Pinkertons in the station?" Ogden asked, incredulously. "I never spotted a one. They're getting better at blending in."

"I hope my men weren't too rough. I don't want to get sued."

"They were gentle as lambs and there were no witnesses. For once, the Pinkertons were discreet."

Mona explained to Alice and Ogden, "My security has been upgraded since the murderer hasn't been exposed. I'm sorry for the inconvenience, but those men are needed for the present."

"How did the reporter know that you would be on the train?" Alice asked.

"He could have followed my car to the train station or someone is feeding him information of my movements."

"I don't think he followed our car, dear," Robert said. "We would have spotted him. Besides your men found a ticket stub in his pocket. He came in on the nine o'clock train. Blodgett was waiting for us."

"Looks like you've got a mole at Moon Manor, old girl," Ogden said.

"Yes, it does," Mona replied, wracking her brain for the names of people who knew she would be boarding the morning train to Cincinnati. Someone from Moon Manor was clearly feeding Mr. Blodgett information. She had a traitor in her midst.

But who was it?

24

The rest of the train ride was uneventful. The group had their tea and buttered toast in the dining car and regrouped in the lounge car to play cards and talk. As more people entered the lounge car, Mona was asked to return to her private compartment by one of the Pinkertons. Reluctantly, Mona and the rest complied and returned to the compartment, spending the rest of the time discussing the wedding.

The train slowed, causing Mona to glance out the window. "We're home." She helped Alice gather her things.

Jamison was waiting at the train station. Mona, Robert, Lady Alice, and Ogden quickly exited the train and entered the motor car. As soon as they were in, Jamison took off for Mooncrest

Farm with another automobile full of hungry Pinkertons following them.

Lady Alice turned to glimpse at the car following. "Goodness, Mona, all the safety measures now. Don't you have any privacy? I don't think King George has this much security."

Ogden said, "I've read that the Vanderbilts, Morgans, and Carnegies all had private subway tunnels built for them in New York so they could travel underground without being detected. They were afraid of kidnappings."

Lady Alice replied, "I think that is a fable."

"I'm hoping that when the murderer of Mabelle is captured, things will get back to normal," Mona said. She couldn't wait to get home. They would have enough time to freshen up and have a small repast in the garden. It was a beautiful day with cerulean skies and the trees were starting to turn, though the air was still warm enough for outside activities without a coat—maybe a light sweater. She just hoped Georgia O'Keeffe wouldn't show up to take a swim. But if she did, it would give Lady Alice and Ogden something to remember.

Mona became excited as Jamison turned into

ABIGAIL KEAM

the long driveway to Moon Manor. She caught a glimpse of Burl, in the gatehouse, calling the mansion to tell Mr. Thomas that Miss Mona and her guests had arrived.

Horses raced with the car along the rock fences while workmen, repairing the hundred-year-old limestone boundaries, waved as the car sped by.

Alice and Ogden commented on the farm. "I don't know if I like spring or fall better," Ogden remarked. "Mooncrest Farm is lovely in both seasons."

Lady Alice rolled down the window and breathed in deeply. "The air smells so fresh. Crisp-like."

"It's the manure in the air," Ogden teased.

"Oh, hush," Lady Alice castigated, laughing. "That's the country for you, Ogden." She took his hand in hers and squeezed, as Ogden looked lovingly at his wife.

Mona caught their intimate glance and turned her face away. It made her long to be with Robert. She closed her eyes, daydreaming of running her fingertips across Robert's lips and his hands unbuttoning her dress, slipping inside the fabric.

The car jolted to a halt and Mona's eyes flew open. "Oh, goodness, I must have dozed off." She got out of the car and greeted Mr. Thomas, Samuel, and Dora dressed in full uniform waiting on the portico.

Jamison opened the car doors and let the others out.

"Welcome to Moon Manor," Mr. Thomas said. "I hope your trip was pleasant."

"It was, Mr. Thomas," Mona assured.

"Very good. Lady Alice and Professor Nithercott. So pleased to see you again. Your trunks will be brought to your room." He motioned to Dora. "Dora will show you upstairs. I will have refreshments ready in a half hour."

"Nice to see you again, Mr. Thomas," Lady Alice said. "We had tea on the train, but some small sandwiches sound good. Some buttery biscuits would be nice as well."

"We will have an assortment of treats," Mr. Thomas assured.

This made Lady Alice very happy. "You know by biscuits I mean cookies."

Mr. Thomas gave a short bow. "I learned my lesson the last time you were visiting, Lady Alice."

Laughing at the memory of being served buttermilk biscuits with gravy for high tea, Lady Alice followed Dora inside.

Ogden pulled Mr. Thomas aside. "I don't think my wife ever realized the biscuits and gravy were a joke. Servants are not as independent minded in England. They would never tease their employers."

"I understand, Professor."

"Well, don't tell Lady Alice the truth. She gets such a kick of telling the story."

"Wouldn't dream of it, sir."

"Thank you." Ogden strode into Moon Manor.

As Mona followed Lady Alice and Ogden, Mr. Thomas gave a short yank on his ear. This was a signal that he needed to speak with her privately. She tugged on Robert's sleeve. "Darling, check your room. Samuel has been moving your things over. I want to make sure you have everything you need."

"Shouldn't he wait until we've left on our honeymoon before my personal things are moved to Moon Manor?"

"I asked him to. Please don't be angry."

"I'm relieved. I think my place is by your side. We're getting married next Saturday. I'm so happy I could bust, and that has me worried. You know that old saying that the Devil comes at your highest triumph?"

"Now who is being cynical? Go check your room, darling. I need to see if there are any urgent messages for me."

"Sure. See you later."

Mona watched Robert bound up the staircase. She turned to Mr. Thomas. "What is it? No one else is dead, is there?"

"Mrs. Aloha Wanderwell, Mrs. Mabel Dodge Luhan, and Miss Georgia O'Keeffe are in the study waiting for you. They wish to have a few words with you before leaving?"

"Leaving?"

"Yes, Miss. They have their travel clothes on."

Mona looked about. "Where's their car?"

"A taxi will be here shortly to pick them up. Their luggage is in the library."

"I'll see them right now."

Mr. Thomas sighed with relief. "Thank you. They have been most trying this afternoon."

Mona went into the study and found the three

ladies together on a couch drinking her best scotch.

Aloha looked amused, Mabel looked irritated, and Georgia looked like the cat, which licked the spilled cream.

"This is a pleasant surprise," Mona lied.

"Not one of my choosing," Mabel said, casting a sideways glare at Georgia.

"Oh?"

Mabel announced, "I'm sorry, Mona, but we are catching the train to New Mexico. We will not be here to attend your wedding."

"Were the accommodations at the Phoenix not to your liking?"

Mabel blurted out, "Georgia has decided she wants to go to Ghost Ranch now and doesn't want to stick around."

"I finished my painting. No need to stay," Georgia said, rising. She reached behind the couch and pulled out a flat rectangle wrapped in brown paper, handing it to Mona. "My wedding gift to you."

"This is the painting you were working on at Robert's cottage?"

Georgia nodded.

"Thank you, Georgia," Mona said, holding the painting. "Should I open it now?"

"Yes."

Mona unwrapped the painting and found herself staring at a pastoral scene with Robert and herself leaning against a white fence with horses grazing in the background. In the far, far background was Moon Manor. For once, Mona felt kindly toward the woman. "It's very beautiful, Georgia. Thank you. I will treasure it."

"I wanted to paint the two of you in the blooming of your love. As time passes, mistakes are made in a marriage. This painting will remind you of how much the two of you loved each other at the beginning."

"I'm very touched. Really, I am. The painting is exquisite."

"Where will you hang it?" Aloha asked.

Mona said, "The painting is so intimate with our expressions. I don't know where to hang it."

Aloha teased, "Yeah, the lust on your face is palpable, Mona. It's making me blush and that's saying something."

Mabel said, "Aloha, must you be so crude?"

"When did you turn into such a crotchety old

biddy, Mabel?" Aloha asked. "Mona's young."

"Are you saying I'm old and past my prime? That I don't feel the primal urge anymore?"

"Do you?"

"The painting is personal. It's not for public rooms. Put it in your bedroom," Georgia suggested, ignoring the squabble between her two friends.

"I think I shall."

Mr. Thomas knocked on the study door and entered. "Ladies, your cab is here to take you to the train station."

Mabel heaved herself up from the couch. "That's us. Let's go, Georgia. New Mexico awaits."

Georgia followed suit with Mona following both ladies to the front door.

"Aren't you leaving, Aloha?" Mona asked.

"No, I'm staying for the wedding, but invite me to stay for dinner. I want to meet Lady Alice."

Mona made a sour face at Aloha who merely grinned back. She stood on the portico and, waving goodbye, watched the two women leave.

Aloha stood behind Mona, waving also.

As soon as the taxi was out of sight, Aloha

said, "I hope you appreciate what Georgia was trying to tell you."

"I do appreciate the painting. It's a very beautiful and thoughtful gift."

Aloha shook her head. "No. No. You don't understand what she was trying to convey. The reason Georgia is going to New Mexico is because her husband is having an affair with a much younger woman. Her mental health is precarious at the moment because of it. Mabel has taken charge until Georgia regains her balance. So, that's why they are leaving now. I don't think she wanted to see your wedding. It would be too painful."

"Mabel alluded to Georgia's marital problems earlier. That's what Georgia meant by 'mistakes are made in a marriage.'"

"Yep. Don't broadcast this around, okay?"

"I won't. It's a very private matter," Mona promised, wondering if she or Robert would stumble in this manner.

Mona didn't think she could bear it if Robert cheated on her.

Then realized she could.

25

"Take that off this instant!" Violet snapped, ripping a veil off Aloha Wanderwell's head. "It's bad luck to put on a bride's veil."

"No need to get snippy, young Violet," Aloha remarked, straightening her hair in the mirror. "Just wanted a look-see."

Violet pushed Aloha away from the mirror. "How can Miss Mona determine how she looks if you are hogging the mirror?"

"Mona, are you going to let your staff talk to me like that?"

"Yes, I am, Aloha. Violet is trying to complete my wedding ensemble, and you are in the way. Get away from the mirror!"

Hoping to diffuse the situation, Lady Alice requested, "Sit next to me, Aloha. I want to hear about you searching for Percy Fawcett in the Amazon."

Violet and Mona cried in unison, "NOT AGAIN!" They had heard Aloha tell this story over a dozen times.

Aloha gave a smug look to Mona and Violet. "Well, it was like this, Lady Alice. I had to learn how to fly a German seaplane, which I flew to Mato Grosso in Brazil. We set up camp at the Descalvados Ranch in Cuiaba to search for Fawcett. Oh, what a time Walter and I had. We made several flights looking for Fawcett, but nothing. Once we even ran out of fuel and had to get the Bororo tribe to help us. They were very leery of us at first, but helped in the end. They literally saved our fannies."

Lady Alice asked, "Did you find any information on the whereabouts of Fawcett?"

"The local people said he went where there were hostile tribes and was killed by them. Anyway, we found no sign of Fawcett or his son."

"Such a shame. Such a shame. He was the last of the great English explorers," Lady Alice murmured, turning her attention to Mona. Seeing her friend try on a new veil, she shot out of her seat. "That one, Mona. That's the one!"

Violet had attached a tulle veil with a satin edge to Mona's tiara and placed it on her head.

Mona swished back and forth looking at it in the mirror. "I like the way it looks. Do you think it is too long? I don't want it to take away from the dress."

"No, it's perfect. Violet, back me up," Lady Alice said.

Mona glanced at Violet, who studied the veil with fastidious eyes. After a moment, Violet beamed and said, "Miss Mona, I think this is the one. It's perfect with the dress and the tiara."

Mona gave one last admiring glance in the mirror. "I like it, too. I think it shall look stunning with the dress."

"Not a day too soon," Aloha said. "Cutting it very close to the wedding to select a veil."

"I've held Violet up. It's been chaos ever since Mabelle died."

"You mean murdered, don't you, Mona?"

Mona gave Aloha a frustrated look. "When are you leaving for the hotel?"

"I'm staying. You need me. I'm good with a gun."

Knowing that Aloha was fascinated with movie stars, Mona coaxed, "Jean Harlow and William Powell are coming to the wedding. They are staying at the Phoenix. Don't you want to be at the Phoenix so you can accidentally run into them?"

"Yes, I know, but they are not coming until the day before the wedding, so I will spend time with you until then."

Lady Alice and Mona exchanged frustrated glances. They had wanted a few days for themselves.

"Tomorrow is the picnic for Mooncrest Farm workers. You will be expected to work like the rest of us."

"You mean you are going to serve the workers yourselves?"

Mona nodded.

"How very democratic of you. Just like Eleanor Roosevelt roasting hot dogs on the White House lawn."

"Don't be snotty, Aloha."

Aloha laughed. She loved to goad Mona about Eleanor Roosevelt. "I'm in. Just tell me what to do."

"Well, in a few moments, we are going out to help the men put up the tables."

Aloha stood and saluted. "I'm your woman."

Mona shook her head, smiling. She could never be angry with Aloha, who was her great friend and always ready to pitch in. Aloha was upbeat, smart, and beautiful. How could anyone resist her charm?

Little did Mona realize that it was a good thing Aloha invited herself to Moon Manor. She would be the key to solving Mabelle's murder.

26

The Mooncrest Farm staff picnic went on without a hitch. As intended, it boosted morale and gave the staff a badly needed break for a day. They had been mowing, painting, gardening, cooking, baking, and cleaning for several weeks. Refreshed and buoyed, the staff readied for the tour and garden party of Mooncrest Farm for the VIPs.

These were employees from the Moon Bank, Moon Enterprises' office, Dexter Deatherage's office, and men from upper and middle management who oversaw the copper mines. Mona was especially concerned with the mining employees. She saw to it that these managers received all equipment and employee benefits requested. Besides the latest gear, the miners needed housing, food that stuck to their ribs, and health care for themselves and their families. Miners were prone to accidents and fainting spells due to bad air circulating in the mines. It was taking Mona longer than expected to get her managers on board with the latest safety precautions and industrial ventilation fans. Mona knew that many of the fans were still in their crates and not hooked up, so she hoped this VIP visit would push her management team to be more sensitive where workers' safety was concerned.

The entire Moon family was present—Mona and Melanie with her two children. They stood on Moon Manor's portico welcoming the visitors.

"Greetings, ladies and gentlemen," Mona said. "Welcome to Mooncrest Farm. We are happy that you could join us on this special occasion— my marriage to Robert Farley, Duke of Brynelleth."

Standing next to Mona, Robert waved and then backed away, giving his bride-to-be center stage.

There was a scattering of applause from the crowd—those from the West seemed especially suspicious of Robert.

"I am Mona Moon. The lovely lady to my right is my Aunt Melanie Moon with my niece and nephew, Meredith and Miles." Mona almost choked on the words, but appearances must be kept.

Melanie smiled and waved to the crowd.

Mona said, "My family is very happy that you are here and hope your stay is a joyous and comfortable one. Let us know if there is anything we can do for you while you visit. Today we are having tours for those who wish to see a working Thoroughbred farm. Also, Moon Manor is open for those who want to see the public rooms, and of course, a high tea will be held in the garden for the next several hours. Each tour will be twenty minutes." Mona pointed to Dotty and Violet. "These ladies with take a group of six people each inside Moon Manor. And if you would like to freshen up, there are several powder rooms downstairs for your use."

The wives murmured in appreciation.

"I have a special delight for you, which I'm sure you will enjoy. Aloha Wanderwell is here and will be giving a short lecture on Brazil and her search for Percy Fawcett."

The audience twittered in excitement.

"Will we be able to go upstairs in Moon Manor?" one lady called out.

"No, I'm sorry. All the upstairs rooms have been locked, and you must enter and leave by the front door. After your tour of Moon Manor, I insist that you visit the garden and enjoy the special treats that Monsieur Bisaillon and his staff have prepared in your honor. Enjoy your time with us and thank you for coming."

Violet raised her hand. "I need six people, please. Just six." Several women crowded about Violet as she led them into Moon Manor.

Dotty did the same and took her ladies on the west side of the house while Violet toured the rooms on the east side of the house. They would both do a quick tour of the kitchen and then switch sides.

Monsieur Bisaillon was told to be on good behavior by Mr. Thomas—no yelling or throwing pans while the guests were present. Mr. Mott put a rope at the kitchen doorway, so the VIPs could lean in to see the kitchen staff working, but not enter.

Violet and Dotty instructed the guests not to

speak to the kitchen staff but observe only. Obliging, the guests were intrigued by the head chef constructing the seven-layer wedding cake as many baked themselves. They were in awe of the cake's construction with the many white dowels. Only with great prodding did they leave the kitchen doorway and continue the tour. Buzzing amongst themselves, they declared they couldn't wait to taste the cake at the wedding reception several days away.

Lastly, the tour ended in the ballroom where all the wedding gifts were displayed as well as five of Mona's fabulous metallic and silk gowns fitted on mannequins. Chattering excitedly at all the lovely things, the guests were then led outside by a Pinkerton, while Dotty and Violet collected more visitors.

While most of the guests were preoccupied with the tours, Mona hid after being waylaid by excited wives asking if her platinum hair color was dyed or if she was related to Jean Harlow. Besieged by the attention, Mona took refuge in the staff dining hall while Melanie took front and center in the garden.

Aloha knocked on the kitchen door, which

Obadiah unlocked and let her in. "Is Mona hiding in here?"

Obadiah thumbed in the direction of the staff quarters.

Aloha grabbed a cucumber sandwich from a serving plate and entered the staff dining area where she found Mona having a glass of lemonade and ginger cookies. "Whatcha doing here?"

"Just needed a quick break. Look." Mona held up a hand. "A woman scratched me trying to shake my hand. Geez."

"Tell everyone they have to wear gloves."

"It would certainly save wear and tear on my hide."

"Better yet, you wear gloves."

"Good idea."

"People are gathering in the garden. It's time for me to give my lecture, and it's time for you to make an appearance. Oh, by the way, your aunt is out there insinuating that she runs Moon Enterprises."

"The woman never quits. Where does she get the energy? I'd like to have some."

"Come on, Mona. Let's go."

Mona took one last sip of lemonade and rose.

She proceeded to a large chest where white cotton serving gloves were kept. She pulled out two pairs, tossing one to Aloha. "Here, better wear these."

Both women headed back through the kitchen and held the side door open for Samuel, who was carrying a tray of pawpaw-flavored, cream pastries to the garden.

Mona cautioned Obadiah before heading out, "Make sure you lock this door after us."

It took Mona and Aloha several minutes to arrive at the garden as they were overwhelmed by well-wishers and autograph hounds. Aloha loved the attention, but Mona found it disconcerting. Finally arriving at the garden, they found Lady Alice and Ogden sitting at a table beneath a black walnut tree.

Ogden said, "I think this VIP visit is having a very good effect on your managers. Everyone seems to be having a grand occasion. We've spent our time people watching and listening to their comments. Very favorable, Mona."

"Have you seen Robert?" Mona asked.

Alice replied, "He, Dexter, and Willie Deatherage, joined the farm tours as narrators.

Should be back soon."

Aloha sat down and fanned herself. "Goodness, today is very warm for fall. I'm perspiring. Should have put on powder. More people are arriving. I think I should have a good crowd for my talk." Gazing about the crowd, a startled Aloha caught her breath and grabbed Mona's hand.

Mona noticed the concern etched on her friend's face. "What is it, Aloha?"

"Who is that man standing next to your aunt? Be nonchalant. Don't let him see you stare."

Casually glancing over, Mona answered, "That is Melanie's fiancé, Enzo Bello."

Aloha patted her forehead with a handkerchief. "I knew it was he. Met Bello in Brazil. He tried to get us to take him into the interior. It was rumored that he captured natives and forced them to work on rubber plantations. No way were we going to oblige him."

"A slaver?"

"He's very dangerous, Mona. Beware. Oh, another thing, he is obsessed with gold."

"Is he now?" Mona said, motioning to a Pinkerton dressed as a waiter.

"When he wasn't rounding up people to enslave, he was prospecting for gold. We wanted nothing to do with him."

The Pinkerton hurried to the table and leaned over as if to remove a glass. "Yes, Miss Moon."

"Tell Mr. Mott to put a man on Mrs. Wanderwell and don't let Enzo Bello get close to her."

The *waiter* nodded. "Right away." He cleaned several tables before discreetly leaving the garden. Within five minutes two more Pinkertons, dressed as staff, entered the garden—one to guard Mrs. Wanderwell and another to keep an eye on Bello.

Seeing that extra security was present, Mona encouraged Aloha. "Go ahead and give your talk. Act as though nothing is amiss."

"Oh, that little shrimp doesn't bother me, Mona, but if Bello is here—that means he's up to no-good. You're the one in danger."

"There's nothing I can do about it now. Let's carry on."

"That's the way," Lady Alice said. "Head up. Chest out. Step forward bravely."

"Ah, the British," Aloha remarked sarcastically, leaving the table. "Talk about slavers."

"What did she say?" Lady Alice asked.

"Aloha said 'talk about beavers,'" Mona replied, rising to join Aloha.

Confused, Lady Alice said to Ogden, "That makes no sense. Why should we discuss rodents?"

"Turn around, dear, and watch the lecture," Ogden replied.

Mona and Aloha went to the podium surrounded by potted yellow and white mums. "Welcome ladies and gentlemen. It is my great pleasure to introduce a dear friend of mine. She is a lady well-known to you since she became the first woman to drive around the world. She's a filmmaker, explorer who speaks eleven languages, author, pilot, and lecturer. She is also the woman who taught me how to shoot a gun. May I introduce to you the fabulous and amazing Aloha Wanderwell."

Everyone clapped, several men whistled, and two photographers snapped away. Mona noticed Michael Blodgett taking notes while sitting with Melanie, her two children, and Enzo Bello. That wasn't good. She strode over to Melanie's table, giving everyone a big smile. "May I join you?"

Both men stood, pulling out a chair for her. Mona thanked them and sat down. Addressing an annoyed Melanie, Mona quipped, "Isn't this fun? Dazzle, Aunt Melanie. Dazzle. Everyone is watching." The six of them clapped and gave bright smiles, giving the guests the impression that the Moon family was stable and united.

Just the impression Mona wanted to make. She subtly peeked at her watch.

An hour to go before the VIP visit would end. Only an hour to go.

27

Mona kicked off her heels and reached for a cup of coffee. Chloe jumped up on the couch as Robert lit the fire in the sitting room before joining Mona. Happy that she had finally been released from Mona's bedroom, Chloe laid her head on Robert's lap and settled in for a quick nap.

Slumped in other chairs were an exhausted Dotty, Violet, Lady Alice, Ogden, and the Deatherages. Aloha was still outside talking with guests and signing autographs.

Monsieur Bisaillon was free to yell now and was shouting orders. Everyone resting in the sitting room could hear him. There was also the banging of the garden tables being taken down as well as noise from the ballroom being cleared.

Dexter cleared his throat. "I think it went well today."

Willie agreed. "I didn't hear one negative comment."

"Neither did I," Violet added. "Everyone was impressed with Moon Manor, although one person said it was smaller than she had imagined. I don't think that is necessarily a negative comment though."

Samuel knocked and entered the room carrying square boxes tied with red ribbons and printed with the Mooncrest emblem. "These are some of the fanciest doggie bags I've ever given out."

"We can't save all the food, but we want to make sure it doesn't go to waste. Monsieur Bisaillon always makes more than we need as a precaution," Mona explained.

"Thus, the doggie bags," Willie said, taking a box from Samuel. "I'm sure not going to say no to one . . . or two." She took another box and untying it, peeked inside. "Oh, Sweet George, all my favorites. I hit the jackpot!" She held the box up so everyone could see inside—cucumber sandwiches, biscuits with grape jam, lemon tarts, tiny strawberry cupcakes, bite-sized glazed donuts, ginger cookies, and powdered wedding cookies.

"Tell the staff to rest after they clean up." Mona pointed to her guests. "We will fend for ourselves tonight. No formal dinner. We'll eat the leftover sandwiches. Leave trays out on the buffet."

"But . . ." Samuel said, thinking of Bisaillon's reaction.

Mona interrupted him. "The cook has been informed. He knows. It's all right."

Samuel looked relieved.

"Tell Mr. Thomas to go to bed now. I saw him earlier and he looked worn out."

"Yes, Miss."

"Thank you, Samuel. Have a nice evening."

Samuel gave out the last doggie *bag* and left the room.

Willie rose. "That's our cue to leave, Dexter."

"So it is. See you both on Saturday at the wedding. Call me if you need anything," Dexter said, giving a short bow.

Willie grabbed his arm. "Come on. You are such a ham."

Dexter and Willie waved goodbye and almost bumped into Aloha entering the room.

"Leaving?" Aloha asked.

Willie said, "It's been a long day. Ta-ta."

Aloha announced, "It has, and I will also be taking my leave of you as well."

"Going so soon?" Mona joked.

"Jean Harlow is coming in tomorrow on the noon plane. I'm making sure I run into her at the Phoenix Hotel."

"As a thank you gift for helping out this week, I made sure your suite is next to hers."

Aloha's eyes lit up. "You are a good friend, Mona."

"And I arranged for the two of you to meet for drinks. Harlow is a big fan of yours."

"Oh, hot diggity-dog. You're a peach. I won't say goodbye. I hate goodbyes."

Mona answered, "Au revoir, then. See you on Saturday."

Aloha rushed up the stairs to gather her things.

Robert patted Mona's knees. "You look all done in, Mona. Take a nap. Ogden and I will check on the cleanup and secure the house. In fact, all four of you ladies go upstairs to your rooms. We'll bring the evening food trays up and place them on the hallway credenzas. That way you can scamper out in your nighties, and no one will be the wiser. It's only an hour or so until dark."

Ogden asked, "What do you femme fatales want to drink?"

"If the kitchen has lemonade, bring a pitcher," requested Violet. "And lots of ice."

"Iced tea for me," Mona said.

Lady Alice added, "I don't care as long as it is wet and cold. I feel unusually warm. You Americans say the weather is getting chilly, but it feels positively tropical to me."

"Chloe, come," Mona said as she rose from the couch and picked up her shoes. "See you all tomorrow. I have a mystery by Agatha Christie to finish." She climbed the stairs with the other women trudging behind her. They each said good night again before entering their rooms.

Mona was exhausted—not physically tired, but mentally worn out. She showered and dressed for the night. Lying in bed, Mona tried to read her murder mystery, but she couldn't concentrate.

She missed Robert being next to her, but he was down the hallway. That was a huge comfort. In a few more days, he would always be with her. No more sneaking around.

Mona turned over in bed ruminating about Mabelle. Why couldn't the sheriff solve this crime? Mona hated that Robert was still a suspect and that nasty rumors floated about town.

Somebody had to have seen something that morning!

Some witness knew who the murderer was!

Why wouldn't he or she come forward?

28

It was Saturday—the day of the wedding. Mona rose early to take a swim before the pool closed for the season. Afterward, she took a hot shower and lathered her skin with exotic oils. Dressed in a terry cloth bath robe, she waited for the hairstylist and manicurist, who were to arrive at eleven.

Violet knocked on the connecting bathroom door and asked, "Shall I get you something?"

"A cup of hot coffee and some dry toast. I'm too nervous to eat anything else."

"Don't worry. You are going to be a gorgeous bride. You're going to have to towel off some of that oil. Otherwise, it will stain the satin."

"I will. I wanted the oil to soak into my skin first. I don't want to look like a prune on my wedding day."

Violet looked sympathetic. "Everything will go as planned. Don't worry."

"Easier said than done." Mona clasped her hands. "Have you seen His Grace?"

"He is downstairs entertaining some last minute arrivals. Don't worry, Mona. It's mostly men telling war stories and drinking all of your bourbon."

Mona looked alarmed at the mention of bourbon.

Violet said, "Your groom is drinking coffee."

Mona sighed with relief.

"I hate to tell you this, but Viscountess Furness is downstairs and demands to see you."

Mona sighed. "Isn't she staying at Robert's? I thought he took care of her."

"The Viscountess doesn't like it at Robert's because he's not there. She wants to be put up at the Phoenix Hotel where everyone else is or here."

"Let the Viscountess come up. I'll work it out with her."

"Okay, but she's in a tizzy."

"I'll take care of it."

A few minutes later, Violet escorted the Viscountess into Mona's presence and closed the bedroom door.

Thelma rushed to Mona and gave her a big hug. "Oh, my dear, but you are sticky."

"I'm doing a skin treatment. This is my wedding day," Mona said, exasperated.

"I know. I know. I arrived late last night and Robert was so kind to let me stay at his house, but no one is there. Everyone is over here. Might I stay? It would be much more convenient for me. I'm just not a solitary person. Everyone knows that about me."

Mona kept her temper in check as the Viscountess had been kind during Mona's trip to England. "Thelma, it is not convenient. Let me put you up at the Phoenix. Everyone is there. Aloha Wanderwell, Alice Roosevelt Longworth, William Powell, Jean Harlow just to name a few."

"I can't stand that Alice Roosevelt. It's always Daddy did this—Daddy, Daddy, Daddy. I get so sick hearing about her family. The only amusing thing she talks about is how much she can't stand her first cousin, Eleanor. I love how she imitates Eleanor and the high-pitched squeaky voice of hers. Now that's funny." The Viscountess pouted. "You must let me stay. I'm in an awful state. Traumatic is what it is. My heart is broken. That witch, Wallis Simpson."

"You mean your best friend?"

"She has stolen David from me."

Mona's mouth dropped open. Laughter bubbled up until it erupted from her mouth.

"I don't think it's humorous, Mona."

Mona put a hand over her mouth to contain her mirth. "I'm sorry the Prince of Wales has left you. I know it must hurt, but this is *MY* wedding day. I can't help except relocate you to the Phoenix Hotel. Now, will you do that for me? I'll have Jamison drive the car to Robert's home and pick up you and your things. Please Thelma, have a heart. I need to get ready for my wedding and the reception."

The Viscountess sniffed. "Very well. I see you don't care about me. I'll go to the hotel and sit in some drab room all by myself."

"Good. That's settled," Mona said, ringing the staff bell.

Samuel answered.

"The Viscountess wishes to relocate to the Phoenix. Please make it happen."

"Would be pleased to assist the Viscountess."

"Thelma, Samuel will show you out."

Taking his cue, Samuel opened the bedroom door wider and said, "This way, Viscountess."

Angry at being dismissed, Thelma swept out of the room.

Before Samuel could follow her, Mona asked, "Were those notes sent?"

"Yes. Sent. Everyone will be here."

"Show them to my study with four chairs lined up before my desk. Have Mr. Mott attend as well, but no chair for him."

Samuel whistled. "One o'clock is getting late for meetings on your wedding day."

"Just do as I ask, please."

"Yes, Miss Mona."

"Thank you."

Samuel left Mona alone in her bedroom as the woman contemplated the one o'clock meeting. It would either fall flat or identify a murderer.

Only time would tell.

29

Mona entered her study at ten after one o'clock, wearing beige trousers with a matching tweed jacket with a gold pin on the jacket lapel. She closed the door.

"What is the meaning of this?" Melanie howled. "And why are these men here? Your note concerned my wedding to Enzo. Are you going to let us have the money now?"

"I asked Mr. Blodgett here to witness what I'm about to say and Mr. Mott to enforce my wishes."

"What is she doing here?" Melanie asked, referring to Dora, who sat next to Enzo Bello.

"Dora is the key to all the recent mischief in Moon Manor."

"I don't know what you mean, Miss Mona. I'm a good girl."

215

"You're a very bad girl, I'm afraid, Dora. You've done nothing but lie."

Dora scrunched up her nose. "Prove it."

Mona dug in her heels. "That's more like it, Dora. Defiant."

Enzo broke in. "Is this meeting about Melanie's marriage to me or not?"

Mona held up a finger. "Give me a moment, Enzo. I'll get to you." She focused her attention on Dora. "You have lied to me about several things. In fact, you've done nothing but lie about Mabelle's death. First you said you never saw Mabelle leave Moon Manor, but in fact you did. You saw her in front of the mansion on her way to the horse barns."

"I admit that I lied. I didn't want to get involved. Don't be mad at me, Miss Mona."

Mona waved Dora's protestations away. "Then you told me some ridiculous story about Mabelle stealing a gold brooch from my Aunt Melanie."

"That did happen."

"It never happened. In fact, it was the other way around. Melanie stole the brooch from Mabelle."

"That's ridiculous. Why would a rich woman steal a brooch when she could buy one?"

"Is it, Dora? You claimed that you heard that story from Meredith. I talked to Meredith on Thursday at the VIP party. She said she had never heard of the gold brooch story and that you two were never friends. The only way you could have heard the story of Mabelle stealing it from Melanie is if Melanie told you that story herself."

Melanie rose up from her chair. "Now see here, Mona."

"Sit down, Melanie. I mean it."

"Well, I never!"

Mona pointed to the brooch on her lapel. "Recognize this brooch, Melanie? It was Mabelle's brooch given to her great great-grandmother as a bribe to keep quiet about a white boy getting her pregnant."

Melanie looked down. "No, I've never seen that pin before."

"I'm telling you one last time. Sit down, Melanie. You're such a bad liar."

Dora blurted out, "I remember now. Miss Melanie told me that story. Yes, she did."

Melanie blurted out, "Shut up, Dora, if you

know what's good for you."

Mona said, "I see that you are starting to sweat, Dora. I know Mabelle didn't tell you the real truth about the brooch. She kept her family life private. She didn't want people to know about the ordeal her great great-grandmother went through. I'm sure Miss Melanie did tell you that made-up story, Dora, just like she told Enzo."

"Now wait a minute," stuttered Enzo, looking between Melanie and Mona.

"I think I figured it out. Melanie was still angry about the loss of the gold brooch and must have persuaded Enzo to steal it for her as she knew Enzo was gold crazy."

"I asked him to purchase it from her. She never wore it. It was going to waste," Melanie explained.

Mona explained, "She wanted it, mainly because she couldn't stand a maid having such an expensive brooch. It didn't take much persuasion for Enzo to agree that he would try to buy, intimidate, or threaten Mabelle to give the brooch to Melanie. After all, he wanted to please his future wife-to-be. She was his meal ticket."

"You can be so cruel at times, Mona," Melanie said.

Ignoring Melanie's insult, Mona continued, "Here's the crux of the problem—why did Mabelle go to the horse barn? If all Enzo wanted was to approach Mabelle about purchasing the brooch, why go to the horse barn? Why not talk to Mabelle in Moon Manor?"

"Yes, why?" Dora asked smugly.

"I never met that woman in the horse barn. I'm innocent of any crime," Enzo proclaimed. He looked to Melanie for support.

Mona waited until Enzo finished. "It was because Dora told her that Virgil Taylor was waiting for her."

"Me? It was never me."

Mona stared at Dora. "You learned Mabelle had a cousin and told her that he needed to see her in the horse barn. Of course, she went immediately only to discover that Enzo Bello was waiting for her. Isn't that right, Enzo?"

Enzo looked defiantly back at Mona. "Like Dora said, prove it."

"I don't have to. Mr. Mott, who is standing behind you, has a full dossier on you, and Aloha

Wanderwell dropped a dime on you as well."

"I met Mrs. Wanderwell many years ago in Brazil. What of it?"

"It wasn't that long ago you met Mrs. Wanderwell and her husband at a rubber plantation. Mrs. Wanderwell has accused you of being a slaver—you kidnapped indigenous people to work on a rubber plantation."

"What if I did?"

"It's morally repugnant."

"Have you looked around the Bluegrass and seen how people with dark skin are treated?"

"You have dark skin, Enzo."

"Please excuse me while I laugh at your hypocrisy. You with your white hair, yellow eyes, and pale skin. You look like a freak. Yeah, a freak of nature is what you are," Enzo blustered.

"Do you admit you killed Mabelle Taylor?"

"You have nothing but supposition."

"That's correct. I can't prove a thing, but with the slaver accusation by Aloha Wanderwell and the mysterious death of a young woman in Brazil after the two of you had quarreled is enough for my aunt to dismiss you as her fiancé. One thing my aunt cares about is how she is thought of in the community. She must save face."

Enzo jumped up. "Dearest, you don't believe this nonsense!"

Melanie backed away from Enzo. "I didn't know about this slave business. I'm afraid I can't be associated with a man who imprisons helpless natives. Not a good thing when Eleanor Roosevelt is crusading for civil rights. I must go with the tide of progress in this matter. The old ways are dying and we must change with the new." She leaned forward toward Mona. "I didn't know Enzo went to meet Mabelle. I never asked him to retrieve the gold brooch. In fact, I had forgotten about it. Ancient history as far as I was concerned. I had no idea where Mabelle might be on the morning in question, but that little alley cat did." She pointed at Dora.

Dora stood up so fast, her chair fell backward. "I didn't know this gold digger was going to kill her. I believed Mabelle stole the brooch, and Mr. Moon gave it to her because he was so vexed at Melanie Moon. That's the story you told me, Miss Melanie. Bello said he was going to pay Mabelle for it and give it to Melanie as a present. I was going to get a fee for setting the meeting up."

Mona felt sad. "Like Enzo said, I can't prove a thing, but I can fire you. You're fired! Mr. Mott, throw her off this property."

Enzo turned to Melanie. "Dear, I forgive you and will give you one last chance."

Melanie rolled her eyes. "Drop dead."

He stood. "This is your last chance, Melanie. I mean it."

Melanie turned her face away from him.

"So be it." He followed Mr. Mott and Dora out of the room.

Mona said, "Don't worry, Melanie. Enzo and Dora will be met by Sheriff Monahan in the hallway. If Enzo's not arrested for the murder of Mabelle, the federal authorities will take custody of him to be deported forthwith. He is an undesirable. Your part in murdering a poor maid will be hushed up."

"Ah, no, Mona. I had no part in the murder of Mabelle. This was cooked up between Enzo and Dora. She probably told Enzo about the brooch and paid him to steal it from Mabelle. I did not ask him to meet with Mabelle. They are both lying about my involvement."

"We'll see what Sheriff Monahan discovers

from his interrogation of Enzo and Dora. What gets me is that you knew Enzo was a two-bit crook when you brought him back from Brazil. Was it to cause a little trouble for me? I betcha you didn't plan on murder though, did you? Caught a tiger by the tail."

"Why am I here?" Mr. Blodgett interrupted. "I can't print this story if there is no proof. It's all she said/he said. I would get sued for libel. I'll have to wait to see if those two are charged and I'm on a deadline."

"Speaking of libel, your editor called me yesterday to comment on a story you wired to your newspaper about me. Naughty. Naughty, Mr. Blodgett. You broke our agreement about printing articles that I didn't approve. You wrote some pretty nasty stuff about me."

Mr. Blodgett blinked heavily, tugging his collar. His eyes looked like enlarged frog eyes through his coke-bottle glasses. "I simply recounted what I was told during an interview."

"Melanie, did you tell Mr. Blodgett evil things about me?"

Melanie sat down and pulled out a powder compact from her purse. Opening the compact, she powdered her nose. "I don't remember what I said. Might have."

"I like to keep notes myself. That's why I had a Dictaphone on the entire time. It recorded our entire conversation. See the little mouthpiece hidden here," Mona explained, as Dotty walked in from the next room and took the wax cylinder out from the Dictaphone hidden in Mona's desk drawer. "Dotty is going to transcribe the conversation and have the transcript in my safe in case you might forget."

"You're going to blackmail us," Blodgett accused heatedly.

"I plan to keep you both in line. You've caused me too much trouble, and I aim to put an end to it."

Blodgett said, "My editor will fight you. He won't stand for it."

"During the course of my talk with your editor, I bought out your contract with the paper. You now work for me."

"What?"

"Here's what is going to go down. You, Mr. Blodgett, have been fired from your paper, and the editor has agreed not to give references to other newspapers. We have several newspapers in Lexington who have acquiesced to interview you for a job on my say so. That way I can keep an eye on you. Enzo's goose is cooked and if Dora knows what's good for her, she will leave town if she's not arrested by Sheriff Monahan. Melanie?"

"What now?"

"You are going to deep-six your Latin Romeo."

"He is such a nice looking man, too. Oh, well, c'est la vie!"

Mona glanced at the clock on the mantel. "If you both would excuse me, I have a wedding gown to slip on. I mustn't be late." Mona rang the bell and Samuel answered. "Have Mr. Mott show these people out."

With those words, Mona walked away, hoping Mabelle's spirit would at last rest in peace.

30

"Governor Laffoon has arrived," Violet said, fussing with attaching the tiara to the veil. "I can hear the police sirens. Goodness, what a racket."

"Make sure he is placed away from Happy Chandler. That man is after the Governor's job."

"Now how can I achieve that when I'm up here with you, Miss Mona?"

Mona threw her hands up. "I don't know. I'm nervous, that's all. My stomach feels like it's doing flip-flops."

"My mother calls it the *wedding day jitters*. You'll feel okay after the ceremony."

A knock sounded on Mona's bedroom door.

Violet hurried over to the door and whispered, "Who is it?"

"Lady Alice."

Violet quickly opened the door and locked it behind Lady Alice. "Who is here?"

"Just about everyone. I took a quick sweep of the garden. Alice Roosevelt is furious that Mr. Thomas won't let her in Moon Manor to see Mona, so she has taken up with Mr. Zhang, who she thinks is the Chinese ambassador."

Mona laughed, as did Lady Alice and Violet. "That dear, sweet little man. I feel sorry for him."

"He'll survive," Lady Alice giggled. "Remember William Donovan? We met him at Viscountess Furness' party."

Mona was startled. "Is he downstairs?"

Violet gave Mona a surprised look. "He wasn't on the guest list."

"Well, he had the engraved invitation, so the Pinkertons let him in. He is hobnobbing with the Viscountess. They are gossiping like mad."

"It's so like Donovan to crash a wedding and with a fake invitation as well. That man is full of tricks," Mona said.

"Shall I tell Mr. Mott to throw him out?" Lady Alice asked.

"Let the man be. He's collecting information for the President. Who else is here?"

"Aloha and Jean Harlow are autographing the guests' wedding invitations. In fact, they plan to sit together at the wedding."

"What about William Powell?"

"The last anyone saw of Mr. Powell, he was languishing against a horse fence and petting your horses. He was also tilting back a silver flask he keeps in his inside pocket. Apparently, Mr. Powell is very much like Nick Charles from *The Thin Man* films."

Mona said, "I hope he holds his liquor like Nick Charles."

"Everything is under control, Mona. The ballroom is set up for the reception. Mr. Thomas has outdone himself with the flowers. The tables look divine—white china, ivory napkins, accompanied by tiny white roses and baby's breath centers. Your table has the red roses. The wedding cake has been placed on its table. It is not tilting, so your nightmare of the cake sliding off its pedestal is not going to happen. Relax. All is butter," Lady Alice said.

"Robert?"

"He is dressed and with Ogden. They are in the garden chatting people up. The only thing left is for you to make an appearance."

"It's time, Miss Mona," Violet said, agreeing.

Mona's eyes teared up.

Violet pleaded, "Please don't start crying. You'll make me cry, too."

"Put it on, Violet. It's time to get this show on the road."

Mona sat still while Violet placed the tiara with the veil on her head.

Violet and Lady Alice stood back to admire Mona.

Mona took one last look in the mirror and said, "I'm ready."

31

At four o'clock, the violinist played the wedding march and everyone stood in Moon Manor's sun-filled garden. Chloe, carrying a white wicker basket dripping rose pedals, trotted down the aisle to Robert who waved a treat for her. After Chloe, Carrying a bouquet of violets, Violet, in a soft blue-green chiffon dress, walked down the aisle as Maid of Honor. Then came a beaming Lady Alice dressed in a dark royal blue chiffon gown carrying white gardenias.

Finally, Mona appeared in a stunning white satin dress, carrying a bouquet of red roses. Her tulle veil flowed to the floor from the late duchess' sparkling tiara. Dexter and Willie Deatherage escorted the beaming bride down the aisle to Robert and Ogden, his best man.

As Dexter gave Mona's hand to her betrothed, Robert shuddered from sheer delight. "Is this a dream?"

"No, now be quiet, so we can get finally get hitched."

Robert grinned. "That's my sassy American cow. My beautiful American cow."

Mona replied softly, "My handsome Englishman."

Robert whispered, "I love you Madeline Mona Moon."

"I love you, too, Lawrence Robert Emerton Dagobert Farley. Come what may, I shall always love you."

"May we proceed?" asked the bemused vicar from Robert's village church in Brynelleth. He had come all the way from England to perform the ceremony in conjunction with the local Episcopalian priest.

Both Mona and Robert blushed while the front row guests, overhearing their comments, twittered.

"Yes, please," Robert said.

Ten minutes later, the minister presented the Duke and Duchess of Brynelleth to the audience.

God Save King George V
And
God Bless President Roosevelt

Albert Benjamin "Happy" Chandler Sr. (1898-1991)

A Kentucky politician who served in the U. S. Senate and Kentucky as its 44th and 49th governor. He also served as Commissioner of Baseball from 1945 to 1951 and is credited with breaking the race barrier with the signing of African American Jackie Robinson for the Brooklyn Dodgers in 1947.

Alfred Stieglitz (1864-1946)

Called the *Godfather of Modern Photography*, Stieglitz was an American photographer who is credited with having the American public accept photography as an art form. Over his 50 year career, he advanced the reputations of many avant-garde artists, including his wife, Georgia O'Keeffe. He published a quarterly magazine called *Camera Work* from 1903 to 1917. Known for its high-quality photographs, some of the most important photographers in the world submitted their work. *Camera Work* is considered by art critics as the most beautiful of all photographic magazines.

Alice Roosevelt Longworth (1884-1980)

She was the eldest child of U.S. President Theodore Roosevelt. Interested in politics, she married Nicholas Longworth (Republican-Ohio) who was the Speaker of the U.S. House of Representatives from 1925 to 1931. Their marriage was unconventional, and both parties had affairs. Their marriage was irreparably broken when Longworth supported William Howard Taft in the 1912 presidential election against Alice's father, Theodore Roosevelt. Alice's only child, Paulina, was sired from an affair with Senator William Borah of Idaho. Paulina died from an overdose in 1955, leaving Alice to raise her granddaughter. Known as a great wit, Alice is famous for saying, "If you haven't got anything nice to say about anybody, come sit next to me." She said of her father's need for attention, "My father always wanted to be the corpse at every funeral, the bride at every wedding, and the baby at every christening."

All Is Butter

Comes from German phrase "alles in butter" which means *everything is okay.*

Aloha Wanderwell (Idris Welsh 1906-1996)

She was a Canadian explorer, author, filmmaker, aviator, travel lecturer, pilot, and screenwriter. At the age of sixteen, Idris responded to an expedition ad promoting "Brains, Beauty, and Breeches—World Tour Offer For Lucky Young Woman." She was hired by Polish explorer Walter Wanderwell (Valerian Johannes Pieczynski) for the position of mechanic and filmmaker. Aloha became the first woman to drive around the world from 1922 to 1927 in a Model T Ford, visiting 80 countries and driving 380,000 miles. She married Wanderwell in 1925. In 1930 she learned to fly a German seaplane that she would later land on an uncharted part of the Amazon River looking for the lost English explorer Percy Fawcett and the Lost City of Z. Instead, she and Walter made first contact with the indigenous Bororo tribe. In 1932, a day before they were to set sail to explore the South Seas, Walter was murdered on their yacht, *Carma*. No one was convicted of his murder. Aloha later remarried, continuing to film her adventures and lecturing.

Bank Closings

In 1932, banks closed their doors when they did not have enough cash on hand to give to their depositors. The panic caused a run on banks and 1400 banks closed. They lost 725 million dollars in total deposits. In 1933, having been sworn in as president only thirty-six hours earlier, President Roosevelt issued Proclamation 2039 on 1 a.m. on Monday, March 6, ordering a suspension on banking transactions for a week. The goal was to give surviving banks time to do inventory and reset. Congress, acting in concert with President Roosevelt, passed the Emergency Banking Act of 1933 on March 9 thus creating the FDIC, which guaranteed depositors' bank accounts up to $5000. Reassured, the public redeposited up to a billion dollars within the month. However, many people still put cash in a tin can and buried the can in the backyard. I know this because my mother was one of many who did not trust banks.

Belle Brezing (Breezing) (1860-1940)

A nationally famous madam of a "bawdy house" in Lexington, Kentucky. Brezing was compromised at the age of twelve by a man who was thirty-six with whom she had a two year affair. Twelve was the age of consent in Kentucky at that time. When fifteen, she got pregnant from one of several men she was seeing and married James Kenney, who deserted her nine days after they were married. Attending her mother's funeral at the tender age of 16 with a baby in her arms, Brezing was locked out of her house by the landlord and her possessions were thrown into the street. The next day she went to work as a street prostitute. At the age of nineteen, she joined Jennie Hill's brothel located in Mary Todd Lincoln's childhood home before opening up her own house, known for its fine furnishings, good food, and excellent liquor. Her house of ill repute was considered one of the finest in the South, and she entertained many famous men. When arrested in 1882 for prostitution, she was given a pardon by Kentucky Governor, Luke P. Blackburn. Margaret Mitchell's husband, John Marsh, working as a reporter for the Lexington Leader, often had breakfast in Brezing's kitchen so he could listen to all the gossip. Many scholars think Brezing is the model for Mitchell's Belle Watling in *Gone with the Wind*. When Brezing died, Time Magazine published her obituary and the Lexington Herald published a front page eulogy. Her home was known as the "most orderly of disorderly houses." During my years at the University of Kentucky, Brezing's house was torn down and the bricks were sold to all comers. I wish I had purchased one.

Bolsheviks

Members of the far-left wing of the Russian Social Democratic Party. They separated from the Mensheviks (Those of the Minority) of the Marxist Russian Social Democratic Labor Party, at its Second Party Congress in 1903. Both factions followed the teachings of Karl Marx and his theories of social and economic emancipation through class conflict in The Communist Manifesto and Das Kapital. Vladimir Lenin became the leader of the Bolsheviks and led them to victory against the White Army (pro-Tzar) in the Russian Civil War in 1917. Lenin most likely ordered the deaths of the Russian Imperial family (the Romanovs) at Yekaterinburg on July 17th, 1918, in order to solidify his power over Russia.

Black Arm Bands
A black armband worn on the sleeve indicates that the wearer is in mourning.

Charles Coughlin (1891-1979)
Father Coughlin was an American Catholic priest and the first of the radio shock jocks. Dubbed the *Radio Priest*, he had an estimated 30 million listeners in his heyday. He was a supporter of FDR's New Deal until he became critical of Roosevelt's banking policies, calling the New Deal the Jew Deal. Coughlin began broadcasting anti-Semitic and conspiracy commentary, supporting Nazi ideology. He used the slogan "Social Justice" to support far-right organizations such as the Christian Front, which was raided in 1940 for plotting to overthrow the government. After WWII broke out, the government considered him an ally of Hitler and threatened to arrest him for sedition in 1942. The Catholic Church made Coughlin step down and he served as local parish priest until his death.

Eleanor Roosevelt (1884-1962)

Mrs. Roosevelt served as First Lady of the United States from 1933 to 1945. During this time, Mrs. Roosevelt worked to expand the rights of working women, WWII refugees, and the civil rights of minorities. She advocated for the U.S. join the United Nations and was appointed as its first delegate. Serving as first chair on the UN Commission on Human Rights, she oversaw the drafting of the Universal Declaration of Human Rights. Roosevelt later chaired President John Kennedy's Presidential Commission on the Status of Women. She was the niece of President Theodore Roosevelt and first cousin to Alice Roosevelt Longworth. Roosevelt married her fifth cousin once removed, Franklin Delano Roosevelt, who became the 32nd President of the U.S. She is considered one of the most admired people of the twentieth century.

Floyd Collins (1887-1925)

A Kentucky cave explorer who became trapped in Sand Cave fifty-five feet underground. His rescue became a national sensation and was one of the first news stories to be reported on broadcast radio. Rescuers were able to bring food and water to Collins until a rock collapse closed the entrance. Now rescuers had to dig him out. Collins died of hypothermia combined with thirst and hunger three days before the rescue team reached him.

Ford Model T
Developed by Henry Ford and sold by his company, the Ford Motor Company from 1908 to 1927. He had the idea of selling to the *common man* instead of the elites and thus had to bring down the cost of the vehicle. Improving on his assembly production line, Ford could sell a car around $850. After selling approximately eleven thousand Model Ts, Ford ceased making other models and remarked about his Model Ts, "Any Customer can have a car painted any color that he wants so long as it is black."

George V (1865-1936)
Grandson of Queen Victoria. Edward VII, died in 1910 making his son, George V, King of the United Kingdom and Emperor of India. It was a well-known fact that King George V was disappointed with his eldest son, David Windsor. He did not consider his son to be *good king material.*

And he was right. David Windsor became Edward VIII and abdicated during the first year of his reign in 1936.

Georgia O'Keeffe (1887-1986)

O'Keeffe is called the *Mother of American Modernism*. A great friend of Mabel Dodge Luhan, she spent much time at the Taos art colony. In 1934, she purchased seven acres from the 21,000 acre Ghost Ranch in New Mexico. Her home is now open to the public for retreats and workshops. O'Keeffe is known for her paintings of Southwestern landscapes and flowers. She is the recipient of the National Medal of Arts and the Presidential Medal of Freedom. Many personal accounts recall Miss O'Keeffe as having a *prickly* personality.

Gesundheit

A German expression that people say after someone sneezes. It means "good health."

Great Depression (1929-1939)

A world-wide phenomenon caused by the U.S. stock market crash in October 1929. The years 1931-1934 were the worst years of the Depres-

sion with an unemployment percentage rate of
15.9, 23.6, 24.9, 21.7 respectively, and even in
1940 unemployment was fifteen percent. President FDR's New Deal programs such as the CCC
and the WPA helped, but it wasn't until WWII
that the country roared out of the Great Depression for good.

Harriet White Fisher (1861-1939)

In 1909, Mrs. Fisher set off in a four-seater, 40
horsepower car to drive around the world. Along
with her maid and a relative, she traveled with a
pet monkey, a Bull Terrier, and a Pug. Since she
did not drive herself, the *First Woman To Drive
Around the World* claim goes to Aloha Wanderwell.
Fisher wrote a book about her adventure titled *A
Woman's World Tour in A Motor*. Fisher testified
against women's right-to-vote in New Jersey in
1913. Thanks for nothing, Mrs. Fisher.

Jean Harlow (1911-1937)

Harlow was an American comedic actress and
one of the first sex symbols of the *talkies*. Known
as the *Platinum Bombshell*, she became one of
Hollywood's biggest stars and is still ranked at
No. 22 on AFI's greatest female stars of the

Golden Age of Hollywood. Harlow died of kidney failure at the age of twenty-six.

Jim Crow Laws (Late 1800s to 1965)

State and local laws enforcing racial segregation in the United States and aiming to disallow any gains made by minorities, especially African Americans during the Reconstruction period after the Civil War. Jim Crow laws were nationally outlawed in 1965.

Juke Joint

An establishment for dancing, gambling, drinking, food, and socializing for African Americans in the southeastern United States. These bars were usually set on the outskirts of town.

Mabel Dodge Luhan (1879-1962)

Luhan was an heiress from a wealthy New York banking family. She became a patron of the arts and is associated with the Taos art colony in New Mexico. She was friends with Ansel Adams, Georgian O'Keeffe, Alfred Stieglitz, Willa Cather, and D. H. Lawrence among other artists and writers. In 1923, she married her fourth and last husband, Anthony Luhan, a full-blooded Tiwa

Native American from Taos Pueblo, New Mexico.

Mammoth Cave National Park

The world's largest cave system with more than 420 miles of surveyed passageways. It is now part of a 52,000 acre national park created in 1941. Human interaction with the cave goes back 5000 years.

Mesopotamia

Historical region between the Tigris-Euphrates river system. Also called the Fertile Crescent. Name covers the modern countries of Kuwait, Iraq, Syria, and Turkey. The area is now referred to as the Middle East which also includes Egypt, Sudan, Saudi Arabia, and other countries.

MI5 (Military Intelligence Section 5)

Founded in 1909 specializing in domestic intelligence. It was originally a joint venture between the Admiralty and the War Office. While MI5 is a nickname, it was officially called Home Section of the Secret Service Bureau. MI6 specializes in foreign intelligence.

Morpheus

Greek god associated with sleep.

Mushy Peas

A British staple made from Marrowfat peas, which are larger and have a higher starch content than most pea offerings. Looks like thick pea soup. Mushy peas are eaten as a side dish or a "sauce" over other foods such as chips.

New Deal

A term taken from Franklin D. Roosevelt's acceptance speech for the presidential Democratic nomination on July 2, 1932. He was voted into the US presidency in November after the public reacted negatively to the ineffectiveness of President Herbert Hoover in regards to the Great Depression, which he said would only last a few weeks in 1929. In 1932, Americans swept the Democratic Party into office with the promise of a *new deal* for the *forgotten man*.

New Deal policies were enacted within the first three months of Roosevelt's presidency, which became known as the "Hundred Days." Agencies such as the Works Progress Administration (WPA) and the Civilian Conservation Corps

(CCC) were established to provide temporary employment. The WPA provided 8.5 million jobs, produced 650,000 miles of roads, built 125,000 public buildings, 75,000 bridges, and 8,000 parks. Also included in the national bills were the Federal Art Project, Federal Writers' Project, and the Federal Theatre Project to document the Great Depression.

Percy Fawcett (1867-1925)
A British explorer, geographer, cartographer, and archaeologist. He was especially interested in South America. He believed there to be a lost city of a great and unknown civilization in the Brazilian jungle. Along with his son, Jack, he mounted an expedition to find this city he called Z. He was last seen in 1925. There were reports of various sightings of him among known xenophobic tribes in the unexplored regions of the Amazon. Many believed these people eventually killed Fawcett and his son. Others thought he died from exposure. Although many expeditions were sent, among them Aloha Wanderwell, no one could find a trace of Fawcett or his son. It is one of the great disappearance mysteries, like that of Amelia Earhart.

Pinkerton National Detective Agency

PNDA is a private security firm created by Allan Pinkerton in the 1850s. The agency performed services ranging from security guarding to private military work. At the height of their power, they were hired by wealthy businessmen to infiltrate unions and intimidate workers. During the Homestead Strike of 1892, the Pinkertons confronted striking steel workers, causing the death of three Pinkertons and nine workers. The Pinkerton Agency is now a division of a Swedish company—Securitas AB.

Prince of Wales

Edward Albert Christian George Andrew Patrick David, formally of the House of Saxe-Coburg and Gotha, now House of Windsor, was born in 1894 during the reign of his great-grandmother Queen Victoria to the Duke and Duchess of York. He was given the title of Prince of Wales on his sixteenth birthday. His father became George V in 1910 and when he died in 1936, the Prince of Wales became king taking the name Edward VIII. Within twelve months, he abdicated the throne in order to marry the American Wallis Simpson. Because she was twice-divorced,

Simpson was considered socially and politically unacceptable as queen. They married in 1937 and self-exiled to France until David's death in 1972.

Prohibition (1920-1933)

In the United States from 1920 to 1933, there was a nationwide constitutional ban on the production, importation, transportation, and, most importantly, the sale of any alcoholic beverage. The anti-drinking movement gained momentum via the formation of the American Temperance Society in 1826. Americans consumed 1.7 bottles of hard liquor per week in 1830, which was three times higher than the amount consumed in 2010. The public grew tired of public drunkenness, domestic violence, vagrancy, and health issues caused by alcohol. By 1920, public opinion wanted the drinking of alcohol banned and Congress obliged. However, there was a backlash—the rise of gangsters who provided bootleg alcohol to illegal speakeasies, which in turn bred more crime such as prostitution and gambling. In 1929 the Great Depression caused the loss of tax revenues, and many officials wanted to reinstate drinking of alcohol so they could tax it. Soon after Franklin Roosevelt was sworn in as president in 1933, he signed the Cullen-Harrison Act that allowed the manufacturing and selling of beer and wine. On December 5, 1933, the 21st Amendment to the constitution totally repealing prohibition was ratified. Alcohol was back in business.

Schadenfreude
A German expression to describe the joy of one person witnessing someone's misfortune.

Sicherheitsdienst (1931-1945)
An independent intelligence agency of the SS and the Nazi Party. It was considered a complimentary organization to the Gestapo secret police. In 1939 it was mainlined into the Reich Security Main Office.

The Intimate Gallery (1925-1929)
A small New York City gallery in the Anderson Galleries Building, Room 303, 489 Park Avenue at Fifty-ninth Street, New York. It was managed by Alfred Stieglitz where he presented new modern artists. He nicknamed the gallery—The Room.

Theodore Roosevelt (1858-1919)

"Teddy" served as the 26th American president. Besides being a politician, he was a naturalist, historian, and author. He was known for his progressive policies such as galvanizing Congress to pass the Pure Food and Drug Act. He is credited with creating our National Parks under which he established 18 U.S. National Monuments, 51 bird reserves, and 150 National Forests putting 230 million acres under Federal protection. He is considered one of our greatest presidents. As for his daughter, Alice Roosevelt, he is quoted as saying, "I can run the country or control Alice, not both."

Viscountess Thelma Furness (1904-1970)

Viscountess Furness, was the American mistress of the Prince of Wales until she was usurped by Wallis Simpson in 1934. She was the aunt of Gloria Vanderbilt and the great-aunt of Anderson Cooper.

U.S. 25

A north-south United States highway that runs from Covington, Kentucky (across from Cincinnati) to Brunswick, Georgia for 750 miles. It is a curvy, hilly two lane road built in the early 1920s as part of the original United States Numbered Highway System. At the time, it was considered an advancement in vehicle transportation that connected the South. It wasn't improved upon until expressways were built under the Eisenhower administration.

Wallis Simpson (1896-1986)

An American socialite, who began an affair with Edward David Windsor, Prince of Wales, and heir to the British throne in 1934. After Wallis' divorce, her beau, now Edward VIII, King of United Kingdom, created a constitutional crisis when he announced his intention to marry the twice-divorced Mrs. Simpson. He abdicated the throne in 1936 in order to marry her. Both Simpson and the abdicated Edward VIII, now Duke of Windsor, were Nazi sympathizers and of great concern to the British government during WWII. The British went at great lengths to suppress intelligence from them. Prime Minister Winston Churchill even threatened the Duke of Windsor if he did not follow orders from the British Government. Eventually, the Duke was appointed Governor of the Bahamas to get him and Simpson out of the Government's hair. After the war, the couple lived in France until their deaths. Simpson is attributed with the quote, "You can never be too rich or too thin."

Wall Street Journal (1889-)
An American newspaper concerning the stock market and business finances in general. They also write exposes. Published by Dow Jones and Company, the paper has received 38 Pulitzer Prizes. It is considered a newspaper of note and still prints daily except for Sunday.

Wilkie Collins (1824-1889)
An English author who wrote *The Woman In White* and *The Moonstone*, considered the first modern English detective novel. He is associated with Charles Dickens as they were great friends and collaborated together on many works. Collins considered Dickens his mentor.

Willa Cather (1873-1947)
An American novelist known for writing about European immigrant pioneer life on the Great Plains. She is known for *O Pioneers, My Antonia,* and *Death Comes for the Archbishop*. Cather won the Pulitzer Prize for *One of Ours* in 1922.

William Donovan (1883-1959)

An American soldier, lawyer, and intelligence officer. Donovan is the only veteran to receive all four of the United States highest awards—the Medal of Honor, the Distinguished Service Cross, the Distinguished Service Medal, and the National Security Medal plus the Silver Star and the Purple Heart. He is best known for serving as the head of the Office of Strategic Services (OSS) during WWII. Another famous alumnus of the OSS was gourmet chef, Julia Child. The OSS evolved to become the Central Intelligence Agency (CIA) after 1945. Donovan was recruited by President Roosevelt in 1934 to "casually" collect information against Nazis living in the U.S. as the States did not have a formal protocol since spying was frowned upon. Secretary of State Henry L. Stimson, under President Hoover, wrote in his memoirs, "Gentlemen do not read each other's mail," and pulled funding for intelligence gathering. Roosevelt knew that Donovan was a loud critic of such action and felt the U.S. needed a formal intelligence department like the United Kingdom's MI6. As soon as the U.S. was attacked in 1941, Roosevelt demanded that he be granted money for such a department with Donovan heading it. Thus began the OSS. Years later, Donovan died after acquiring dementia, taking all his secrets with him to the grave. A statue of Donovan stands in the CIA Headquarters lobby.

William Powell (1892-1984)

Powell was an American actor who was nominated three times for the Academy Award for Best Actor. He was better known for playing private detective Nick Charles in *The Thin Man* films in which he co-starred with Myrna Loy. Powell was the last consort of Jean Harlow who died of kidney failure at the age of 26 in 1937.

Books By Abigail Keam

Josiah Reynolds Mysteries

Mona Moon Mysteries

About The Author

Abigail Keam is an award-winning and Amazon best-selling author. She is a beekeeper, loves chocolate, and lives on a cliff overlooking the Kentucky River. Besides the 1930s Mona Moon Mysteries, she writes the award-winning *Josiah Reynolds Mysteries*, *The Princess Maura Tales* (fantasy), and the *Last Chance For Love Series* (sweet romance).

Don't forget to leave a review!
Tell your friends about Mona.

Made in the USA
Monee, IL
26 January 2023